MAGGOT MOON

MAGGOT MOON

Sally Gardner

HOT
KEY
BOOKS

First published in Great Britain in 2012 by Hot Key Books
Northburgh House, 10 Northburgh Street, London EC1V 0AT

A CIP catalogue record for this book is available from the British Library.

Hardback ISBN: 978-1-4714-0004-9
Export paperback ISBN: 978-1-4714-0005-6

1

Typeset by Palimpsest Book Production Limited,
Falkirk, Stirlingshire
This book is set in 11pt Sabon

Printed and bound by Clays Ltd, St Ives Plc

FSC

Hot Key Books supports the Forest Stewardship Council (FSC),
the leading international forest certification organisation, and is committed
to printing only on Greenpeace-approved FSC-certified paper.

www.hotkeybooks.com

For you the dreamers
Overlooked at school
Never won prizes

You who will own tomorrow.

One

I'm wondering what if.

What if the football hadn't gone over the wall.

What if Hector had never gone looking for it.

What if he hadn't kept the dark secret to himself.

What if . . .

Then I suppose I would be telling myself another story.

You see, the what ifs are as boundless as the stars.

Two

Miss Connolly, our old teacher, always said start your story at the beginning. Make it a clean window for us to see through. Though I don't really think that's what she meant. No one, not even Miss Connolly, dares write about what we see through that smeared glass. Best not to look out. If you have to, then best to keep quiet. I would never be so daft as to write this down, not on paper.

Even if I could, I couldn't.

You see, I can't spell my own name.

Standish Treadwell.

Can't read, can't write,

Standish Treadwell isn't bright.

Miss Connolly was the only teacher ever to say that

what makes Standish stand apart is that he is an original. Hector smiled when I told him that. He said he personally had clocked that one straight away.

'There are train-track thinkers, then there's you, Standish, a breeze in the park of imagination.'

I said that again to myself. 'Then there is Standish, with an imagination that breezes through the park, doesn't even see the benches, just notices that there is no dog shit where dog shit should be.'

Three

I wasn't listening to the lesson when the note arrived from the headmaster's office. Because me and Hector were in the city across the water, in another country where the buildings don't stop rising until they pin the clouds to the sky. Where the sun shines in Technicolor. Life at the end of a rainbow. I don't care what they tell us, I've seen it on the TV. They sing in the streets – they even sing in the rain, sing while dancing round a lamp post.

This is the dark ages. We don't sing.

But this was the best daydream I'd had since Hector and his family vanished. Mostly I tried not to think about Hector. Instead I liked to concentrate on imagining myself on our planet, the one Hector and I had invented. Juniper.

It was better than being worried sick about what had happened to him. Except this was one of the best daydreams I'd had for a long time. It felt as if Hector was near me again. We were driving round in one of those huge, ice-cream-coloured Cadillacs. I could almost smell the leather. Bright blue, sky blue, leather seats blue. Hector in the back. Me with my arm resting on the chrome of the wound-down window, my hand on the wheel, driving us home for Croca-Colas in a shiny kitchen with a checked tablecloth and a garden that looks as if the grass was Hoovered.

That's when I became vaguely aware of Mr Gunnell saying my name.

'Standish Treadwell. You are wanted in the head-master's office.'

Frick-fracking hell! I should have seen that coming. Mr Gunnell's cane made my eyes smart, hit me so hard on the back of my hand that it left a calling card. Two thin, red weals. Mr Gunnell wasn't tall but his muscles were made out of old army tanks with well-oiled army-tank arms. He wore a toupee that had a life of its own, battling to stay stuck on the top of his sweaty, shiny head. His other features didn't do him any favours. He had a small, dark, snot-mark moustache that went down to his mouth. He smiled only when using his cane – that smile curdled the corner of his mouth so that his dried-up leech of a tongue stuck out. Thinking about it, I am not sure the word smile is right. Maybe it just twisted that way when he applied his mind to his favourite sport, hurting you. He wasn't that worried where the cane landed as long as it hit flesh, made you jump.

You see, they only sing across the water.

Here the sky fell in long ago.

Four

But the thing that really scratched at me was this: I must have been so many miles away. I didn't even see Mr Gunnell approaching, although there was a runway between me and his desk. I mean, I sat at the very back of the class – the blackboard could have been in another country. The words were just circus horses dancing up and down. At least, they never stayed still long enough for me to work out what they were saying.

The only one I could read was the huge red word that was stamped over the picture of the moon. Slapped you in the gob, that word did.

MOTHERLAND.

Being stupid, and not being anything that fitted neatly on to lined paper, I'd sat at the back of the class long enough to know I'd become all but invisible. Only when Mr Gunnell's army-tank arms were in need of some exercise did I come into focus.

Only then did I see red.

Five

There was no getting away from it. I'd got lazy. I'd got used to relying on Hector to warn me of oncoming doom. That daydream made me forget Hector had disappeared. I was on my own.

Mr Gunnell got hold of my ear and pinched it hard, so hard my eyes watered. I didn't cry. I never cry. What's the use of tears? Gramps said that if he were to start crying, he didn't think he would stop – there was too much to cry about.

I think he was right. Salty water wasted in muddy puddles. Tears flood everything, put a lump in the throat, tears do. Make me want to scream, tears do. Tell you this, it was hard, what with all that ear pulling. I did my best to keep my mind on Planet Juniper, the one

Hector and I alone had discovered. We were going to launch our very own space mission, the two of us, then the world would wake up to the fact it was not alone. We would make contact with the Juniparians who knew right from wrong, who could zap Greenflies, leather-coat men and Mr Gunnell into the dark arse of oblivion.

We had agreed we would bypass the moon. Who wanted to go there when the Motherland was about to put her red and black flag in its unsoiled silver surface?

Six

Mr Gunnell didn't like me. I think it was personal. Everything is personal with Mr Gunnell. I was a personal affront to his intelligence. I was an affront to his sense of order and decency. Just to make sure everyone got the message about the affront that was me, he pulled my tie undone. He had that smile on his face, the tongue sticking out one, as he closed the classroom door behind me.

I didn't have a problem with the caning. Or with the fact that my hands still smarted. I had a small problem with the ear pulling. I was only a tiny bit worried about the headmaster. I didn't know then about the trouble, or how deep it went.

But maybe I got an inkling of it the moment Mr

Gunnell pulled my tie undone, the git. You see, I can't do up my tie, and he knew it.

That tie had not been untied for a personal record of one year. That was the longest time I had ever managed to keep the knot intact. In fact the fabric had become so shiny that it moved with no problem just wide enough for my head to slip through and then close up as neat as a whistle at the top, so I looked spick and span. I mean, that was the idea. It had stayed this way because of Hector. He wouldn't let any boy mess with me. The days of torment I had believed to be behind me. That fricking, undone, hangman's rope of a tie made me feel like sliding down the wall on to the floor and giving up, letting the tears for once get some exercise. For there was one thing I couldn't do: go to the headmaster's office without a tie. I might just as well throw myself from the window head first. Say it came undone on the way down. Say due to concussion from the fall I had forgotten how to tie a tie.

I think I knew, if I was honest, then and there, that this was not just about the tie and the loss of a knot. It was the loss of Hector I couldn't stand. If only I knew where they had taken him. If only I knew he was all right, then maybe the knot in my stomach – the knot which got tighter every day – would go away.

Seven

Hector said the tie stood for something different. It was just the same as a collar round a dog's neck. It said you were a part of something more than you alone would ever be. Hector said a uniform was a way of making us all the same, just numbers, neat boy-shaped numbers to be entered in a book. Hector wasn't a neat number and I think they might have rubbed him out, but I can't be sure of that. What I knew was that Hector was right. The knotted tie represented survival.

Now I was stuck, tie undone, my shirt buttoned wrong, my shoelaces a dead loss. I was a mess.

Eight

The corridor smelled of disinfectant, milk, boy's pee and polish. The striplights looked to me like loneliness. They were too bright, they revealed everything. They made the emptiness ten times worse, showed me there was no Hector. A glass door banged and Miss Phillips, one of the school wardens, came out of her office carrying a cup.

'What are you doing, Treadwell?'

She had a hard, no-nonsense voice but I'd seen her in the queues like everyone else, getting a little extra on the side. She looked down the corridor and up at the camera that went round like clockwork. She waited until the all-seeing eye was turned elsewhere then without a word she tied my tie, re-buttoned my shirt. She checked the camera, put her finger to her lips and waited for it to turn back on us before saying in the same, no-nonsense voice, 'Good, Treadwell. Now that is how I expect you to arrive at school every day.'

Never would I have thought that the hard-boiled Miss Phillips had such a soft, sweet centre.

Nine

The headmaster's office had a seat outside, a long bench, wood hard, bum sore, and just a bit too high. I reckon that was the genius of the seat because you ended up sitting there looking small and less of anything, with your feet dangling and your knobbly knees blushing red. And all you heard was the sound of your classmates hardly daring to breathe. I sat there waiting for the bell to ring, which meant Mr Hellman will see you now. I sat and waited, time drip-ticking away.

Before Hector came to this school, I hated it. I believed it was invented just so the bullies, with brains the size of dried-up dog turds, could beat the shit out of kids like me. A kid with different-coloured eyes: one blue eye, one brown, and the dubious honour of being the only boy in the whole of his class of fifteen-year-olds who couldn't spell, couldn't write.

Yes, I know.

Standish Treadwell isn't bright . . .

How many times did the jerk-off bully boys sing that to me, egged on by the glory-arsed leader of the torture lounge, Hans Fielder. He knew he was important. Head Perfect, the teacher's pet. He wore long trousers, as did the rest of his gang. Tell you this for a bucketful of tar: there weren't many in our school who wore long trousers. Those that did thought themselves up there with the greats. Little Eric Owen wore shorts like the rest of us but he made his shorts longer by doing everything Hans Fielder required of the runt. If Little Eric was a dog he would have been a terrier.

His main duty was to see which way I was heading home every day and give the signal to Hans Fielder and his merry men. The boys needed something to get their teeth into. The chase would be on. I ended up being caught and beaten every frick-fracking time. Don't think I didn't give as good as I got, because I did. But I didn't stand much of a chance when there were seven of them.

It was the day I first met Hector. They had me cornered

under the old railway tunnel near the school. Hans Fielder thought he'd caught me good and proper, that there was no escape unless I wanted to risk being killed, for at the end of the tunnel was a sign. You didn't have to be able to read it to know what it said. It had a cross and skull bones on it, which meant keep out or you're dead.

That day, down there in the stinking tunnel with Hans Fielder and his gang of nasties jeering and throwing stones at me, I came to the rapid conclusion that it might be safer to run into the long grass behind the sign and take my chance with the devil. There was no barbed wire or anything like that to fence it off. That notice alone had the power of a thousand scarecrows.

I ran down the tunnel for all I was worth, past the sign into what I was certain would be a firing range. At least it would be over quickly. Mum and Dad were gone and Gramps . . . well, I didn't let myself think about Gramps, not right then. Because Gramps was the only person that still pulled at the gravity in me. I glanced over my shoulder, expecting to see Hans Fielder and his frickwits following me. What I saw was a murky group of lads drifting away.

I stopped by a huge oak tree, out of breath, dizzy. It

was only when my breathing became more steady that I realised what I'd done. I waited some time. If the Greenflies turned up I would put my hands up and give myself in.

I sat down, my heart an egg bumping against the side of a pan of boiling water. It was then that I spotted it. A red football. Deflated, yes, but whole. I stuffed it in my school bag, a reward for my bravery. Not only that, but as I went further along the disused railway track I found raspberry bushes groaning with fruit. I took off my shirt, tied the sleeves together and filled it up until it couldn't take another raspberry. All the time I was expecting to feel a Greenfly's hand on my shoulder.

By now I was near the wall that runs along the side of the railway track. A word to describe that wall would be *impenetrable*. See. I might not be able to spell but I have a huge vocabulary. I collect words – they are sweets in the mouth of sound.

The wall was built so high that Gramps and me, whose garden backed on to it, couldn't see over the fricking thing. You wouldn't know there was a wild meadow hidden behind it filled with flowers. Butterflies were doing the fandango like nature was having a ball and keeping the VIP list all to herself. I was seeing it for the first time and, cripes, it was eye-bending in its beauty. Well, I thought, if all mankind disappeared down a hole I knew who would be holding the celebration party.

Why stop now, Standish? You have the raspberries, the football – why not the flowers?

Twerp. Only then did it dawn in my daydreaming head that I hadn't the foggiest idea how I was going to get over the wall. I was up shit river with a hole in the boat and sinking fast. I mean, I couldn't climb the wall. It wasn't the height that concerned me, it was the glass at the top, the artery-cutting kind. You wouldn't be able to get over that wall and still claim to have hands.

Frick-fracking hell. There were two choices: I would have to go back the way I came, which I wasn't doing; and the other . . .

. . . Standish, go on, tell me the other.

Ten

The brick wall stops at the end of our road, where there is this huge pointless palace that sits at the top of the hill. I was certain, when I was small, that it was made from a giant's toy building set because it was out of scale with everything else. Gramps said it was cursed.

What I'm telling you now happened for real. A long way back, some bright spark thought to commemorate a queen or a battle – I can't remember which, both being as forgotten as the other. According to Gramps, who liked to study local history, the hill, many moons ago, had on the top of it a deep well, known for its magical healing water and guarded by three witches. They decreed nothing should ever disturb this spot and if the well was tampered with in any way then the land would be cursed.

This was before those wise witches were dragged away to the stake house.

Years later, a geezer with wheelbarrows of money and a queen or a battle to remember went right ahead and filled in the well, and built the atrocity.

The first people's palace burned down on its opening day. Then, as if that didn't make the witches' point fair and two corners square, the man with the wheelbarrows of money went and built the ugly bugger up again. A sort of two fingers to the superstition. Gramps said, the thing with witches is they can afford to play the long game. That glass eye of the ugly old palace was still watching from beyond the meadow.

Why was I thinking about this when I was stuck on the wrong side of the wall refusing to let go of the flowers, the shirt with the raspberries, or the squashed football? Because it gave me time to calm down, to think, and in that thought I found my means to escape.

Before he and Mum disappeared, I'd once heard Dad talking to Gramps about a tunnel they'd dug from the air raid shelter during the war. It led into the park. When they realised I was in the room, they started speaking in the Mother Tongue so that I wouldn't understand.

What I have discovered about languages is this: when you are not good at spelling or reading you become a whizz at hearing words. They are like music, you can squeeze out the essence of them. All I had to do was empty my mind, tune into the delivery of the speech and nine times out of eight I had it spot on the mark.

I tell you this for nothing, I could have yelped for joy when I finally found the hatch to that tunnel. There it was, buried under a tangled carpet of greenery. It had been hidden for such a long time that it took all my strength to make nature relinquish what she believed belonged to her.

I felt like bleeding Santa Claus when I put my bounty on our kitchen table.

Gramps was astonished.

'Do you know, lad, there are two things I wish for at the moment. First, that I knew how to make raspberry jam and second, how the flipping hell we make your one and only shirt white again.'

Once I might have said someone heard his prayers and answered them. But now I know it was more random than that. Hector and his family had just moved in next door. Gramps was sure they were spies and if they were, he reckoned they would know how to make a raspberry-stained shirt white. And that's how it all got started.

Eleven

Gramps always made me feel safe. The walls of our house may have been shaky, but they weren't see-through – Gramps made sure of that. He was a silver fox, cunning. He stood tall and proud, always told me he owned nothing but his dignity and he wasn't about to give that away to no one. To no creed, to no church, to no dogma. Nothing passed the twinkle in those grey eyes of his. He saw a lot, said a little.

When our new neighbours moved in, he said he wasn't about to take over a bowl of sugar.

'Sugar?' I said. 'Why would you do that? It's like gold dust.'

Gramps laughed. 'Before the war when the streets were lined with smart, un-bombed houses, you would

be neighbourly. If someone was in want, you gave.'

That struck me as a sensible idea, but there was no one else in our street of derelict houses who you could give anything to. Gramps told me the Lushes were spies. I knew that was another way of saying he didn't want anyone living there. The house had belonged to my parents before they became non-existent. It made their disappearance more final. Dotted their eyes, made the question mark next to the Why that much bigger, that much harder to avoid. At that time, Mum and Dad had vanished over a year back. There were many unexplained disappearances: neighbours and friends who like my parents had been rubbed out, their names forgotten, all knowledge of them denied by the authorities.

It had struck me then that the world was full of holes, holes which you could fall into, never to be seen again. I couldn't understand the difference between disappearance and death. Both seemed the same to me, both left holes. Holes in your heart. Holes in your life. It wasn't hard to see how many holes there were. You could tell when there was another one. The lights would be switched off in the house, then it was either blown up or pulled down.

Gramps always suspected that the main informers in our neighbourhood lived in the rooster-breasted houses at the top of the road, the other end from the palace. These were the sound, untouched homes specially reserved for the Mothers for Purity. Like Mrs Fielder and her crones. They did sterling work for the Greenflies and the men in black leather coats, spying on their neighbours in return for baby milk and clothes, all those little extras that the mere, half-starving, non-cooperating citizens like us queued for every day.

I asked Gramps why would spies know how to get a raspberry-stained shirt white.

'They wouldn't,' he said, 'but the woman might.'

I didn't think that made much sense but Gramps had been very grumpy lately, ever since the family had moved in next door. Grumpy in a crotchety way, which Gramps hardly ever was.

'Life has become more complicated,' he said.

I didn't know then that old silver fox had a bushy tail. He'd kept that well hidden.

Twelve

It was my idea to take the flowers and a bowl of raspberries round to our neighbours as a present. I thought it might help with the shirt business. By the time we had agreed to do it, the curfew siren had sounded. We heard one of the Greenflies' armoured patrol cars make its first round of the evening, so the street was out of the question, and the only means of paying a visit to any of the other houses without being seen was to go down to what I called Cellar Street. Cellar Street was nothing more than a series of holes pick-axed through the basement walls of the houses. A supply path. It was the best way of collecting wood and stuff from the derelict buildings without being seen.

I never liked it down there. It gave me the creeps. It

was dark, smelled of damp. There were lots of things to bump into.

We went up the steps that lead to the cellar door of what used to be my parents' house. I could tell what was behind that door without it being opened. Red-flowered wallpaper with bulging baskets of fruit, red wooden panelling which ran round the lower part of the kitchen and was red only because that was the colour of the paint that had fallen off the back of a lorry. Gramps had rescued the light from the old police station after it was bombed. All this and more was known to me about the house I was born in.

Nevertheless, we knocked politely.

Thirteen

There was a loud silence, then the door opened a little.

'Yes, what do you want?' said a man.

He spoke our home language well, with only a slight accent, but you could tell it wasn't what his tongue was used to. He was, by the sound of him, a paid-up member of the Motherland, the real McCoy. Tell you this for a pocketful of dirt, you don't see many of them – civilians, that is – in Zone Seven. It was quite a shock to me. It struck me that maybe Gramps was right about this spy business after all.

The man was coat-hanger thin, with a shock of grey hair. He had grey, bushy eyebrows, the only barricades against a large expanse of wrinkled forehead that threatened to tumble down in an avalanche of anxiety over the rest of his features.

'We have no food, we have no valuables,' he said, his voice wavering. 'We have nothing to give you, nothing.'

I thought Gramps would harden when he realised this man was from the Motherland. But his voice was soft.

'I am your neighbour, Harry Treadwell, and this is my grandson, Standish Treadwell,' he said, holding out a hand.

The man slowly opened the door.

Sitting at the table, just like my mother used to sit, was a thin, pretty woman and opposite her, where I used to sit, was a boy of my age. Handsome, straight-backed, dark blonde hair and green eyes.

'I just thought,' said Gramps, 'that I would see if you were settling in all right.'

I took the flowers and the small bowl of raspberries to the woman. She accepted the flowers and buried her face in the blooms. When she turned to me again there was golden pollen on her nose and a tear rolling down her cheek. She touched the bowl of raspberries with trembling hands.

I was aware all this time that the boy was staring at me and I wanted to stare right back at him but I didn't, not at first. I felt my cheeks to be red, felt awkward, unable to gauge the scene before me. Finally, in defiance, I turned to him, imagining that, like my classmates, he would find me strange, with my blemish of impurity.

What odd eyes you have.

What odd words you spell.

But his face was serious. He stood up. He was taller than me. He was not nervous like the man and the woman. Self-assured, he walked up to me.

'Thank you,' he said. 'My name is Hector Lush and these are my parents.'

I knew him.

But I knew I didn't. I had never seen him before.

Gramps hadn't moved from the cellar door. He just stood there watching, taking in all he saw. Then suddenly he turned tail and went back the way he had come. He called to me when he was at the bottom of the cellar steps.

Fourteen

It didn't take us long to gather what we needed from our house, which was basically my dad's revolver. It had the luxury of a silencer, stolen from a dead Greenfly. We went back up again into what once had been my kitchen. This time Gramps didn't knock. Mr Lush saw the gun and rushed to his wife's side.

Hector smiled. 'Are you going to kill us?' he asked, calmly.

Gramps was unused to being polite, and the rigmarole of manners didn't really interest him much. He said nothing, and taking aim, shot the first rat as it ran along the skirting board, then the second one, then the third . . . he stopped when he had shot seven of the buggers.

Numbers mattered to Gramps. Seven dead rats was something the king of the rats would respect. Shoot one rat and all his relatives will come looking for you; shoot seven and they understand you mean business.

Fifteen

We took the Lushes through Cellar Street, back to our home. They stood in Gramps' neat kitchen, amazed. He had his system for survival down to a fine art. Nothing was wasted, everything collected and stacked with the order of a librarian. I helped him lay the table, each item cracked, broken, mended, cracked, broken, and mended again until it had an originality all of its own.

'Standish,' said Gramps, 'the sloe gin.'

The minute he said that I knew he trusted the Lushes. But he wasn't going to say so and he never did.

We all sat round the table. Both me and Gramps had finished our soup and were mopping our bowls with our homemade bread. When we looked up the Lushes hadn't even started theirs.

'It's cold cucumber,' said Gramps. 'I made the bread this morning. Eat up.'

'Do you mean you will share this with us?' said Mrs Lush, her face translucent, her eyes fishes, swimming in puddles of tears.

'Yes,' said Gramps. 'It will get you out of jail.'

'What do you mean?' asked Mr Lush.

'Stop you starving to death,' he said. 'There is a reason why you are in Zone Seven. I don't need to know it. If we turn on each other and you all die then they have won. If we stay together we are strong.'

'You know that not all from the Motherland agree with what is being done in her name,' said Mr Lush.

'Of course,' said Gramps.

'We thought you would be suspicious of us, think we were informers.'

'Eat up,' said Gramps. He raised his glass. 'Let's drink a toast: to new beginnings – and moon landings.'

Sixteen

That night the Lushes stayed in our house. For the first time since my parents left I slept in my old bedroom, Hector on a mattress on the floor.

Only as I was falling asleep did I remember we still hadn't tackled the raspberry-stained shirt.

I hadn't slept through the night once since my parents went. Gramps was exhausted. It was only because of Hector that I began to sleep properly. Mr Lush and Gramps agreed the next night to knock the doorway through the wall that joined our two bedrooms so we might be together. I don't remember anything being discussed about knocking more doorways between the two houses, it just happened. Gramps, me, Hector and Mr and Mrs Lush all started

to eat together, and bit by bit we stayed together. We were a good family.

Mr Lush told us he was an engineer. He had refused to work on a project in the Motherland but what it was, he wouldn't say. Mrs Lush was a doctor who had refused to eliminate the impure. Which was really very good for Gramps, me and the impure, for they all ended up exiled to Zone Seven.

Seventeen

I rocketed off my seat when the bell rang. Slicked my hair down, took a deep breath, knocked on the door and went in. Mr Hellman was standing up. He clicked his heels together, although I couldn't see his heels as they were under his desk.

Then his arm shot out, scaffold-pole straight, and this glazed look came into his eyes as he said, 'Glory to the Motherland.'

I half-heartedly raised my arm – but didn't – and then I heard a cough. This cough was not coming from Mr Hellman. It was coming from a man sitting in the corner of the room, a man in a black leather coat. He looked as if he was made up out of a geometry set, all triangles and straight edges. His face was hidden by a hat. It wasn't at a rakish angle, not like they wear them in the land of Croca-Colas. No, this hat was knife sharp with a brim that could slice a lie in half. He wore black-framed, eye-socket-fitting sunglasses. It was gloomy in the office. I wondered what he could see and what he couldn't. Tell you this much: he stood out like a sore thumb in a thunderstorm. He meant business, but whose or what I couldn't figure.

What, I wondered, is he doing here? I thought maybe he was checking up on Mr Hellman, though I doubted it. Mr Hellman's great claim to fame was that cheap chrome watch of his. It had been awarded to those couples who have had eight or more children. You see, no one wore a watch in Zone Seven unless they were important. Everyone else sold theirs on the black market long ago. How did I know that Mr Hellman's was a cheap watch? Well, I didn't, not until I saw Mr Lush's. That watch saved us.

Last winter was the coldest I could remember, ever. Gramps said he had never known one as cruel and he had known a fair few. Gramps had called it the revenge of General Winter. That General wasn't on our side, that much I can tell you.

If it hadn't been for Mr Lush's watch we would have been goners. We were down to one church candle to light the house and all that was left to eat was potato peel. One morning, when everything was frozen up including the bog, we were all sat round the kitchen table, Gramps working out what else he could use for firewood to keep the stove alight, when Mr Lush suddenly left the room. We heard him over our heads lifting floorboards. I was thinking we can't burn those, the house might fall down. Mrs Lush said nothing. She just started to twist her hands round and round. When Mr Lush came back into the kitchen he handed Gramps something wrapped up in a cloth.

He said quietly, 'You know what to do with it, Harry.'

Gramps carefully unwrapped it. Fricking hell. It shone bright as a star, that watch did. It turned out to be real gold, solid as Sunday.

Gramps turned it over. He studied the inscription on the back for a long time and said nothing. Mr Lush was worried-white. I could tell that Mrs Lush had stopped breathing.

It was an eternity before Gramps said, 'If we can grind off the words it will get us out of jail.'

Mr and Mrs Lush took a deep breath and nodded.

'Thank you, Harry,' said Mr Lush.

Later I asked Gramps what it said on the back of the watch. He refused to tell me.

We still have some of the flour, rice, oats, candle oil and soap, all bought on the black market. So I knew Mr Hellman's watch was worthless. It wouldn't even buy him a candle to light his grave by.

Eighteen

Mr Hellman started twiddling his thumbs. He had hairs sprouting out of the back of his hands. Black hairs like spider's legs.

But that was by the by, that was just a distraction, like the watch itself. You see, there was so much wrong with this picture. For a start, the headmaster wasn't full of wind and bustle. He looked like a deflated Zeppelin – all the hot air gone.

The knot in my stomach told me that this leather-coat man was here to see me, and I was thinking really, really fast about what kind of trouble I might be in. I went through a list.

Was it the TV we'd retuned?

Was it about the two hens we had at the bottom of the garden?

Was this about Hector?

'Standish Treadwell?' demanded the leather-coat man.

I nodded. I tell you something – I was standing up straight then.

'Do you know what today is?'

Of course I knew what day it was – it was Thursday, and we would have spam fritters for supper with the two eggs we'd been saving. But I knew what he wanted me to say – I mean, you would have to be really stupid not to know what day it was.

So I said nothing.

Nineteen

'Standish Treadwell.'

Why was he saying my name again, and what was in the folder he was holding?

'How old?'

'Fifteen, sir.'

'Fifteen.'

I didn't like this repeating business. I looked at Mr Hellman but he wasn't joining in.

'Fifteen,' said the leather-coat man. 'With the writing age of a four-year-old and the reading age of a five-year-old. Do you know what happens to children with impurities?'

'Yes, sir.'

I knew you got sent to another school, far away. It

happened to Mike Jones, he of the funny legs. He'd never come back. Gramps told me Mrs Jones, his widowed mother, had as good as lost her mind over the business. Still I didn't say anything.

'Standish.'

What was wrong with this leather-coat man that he kept saying my name?

'A strange name.'

Shit. I wished I had been called John, Ralph, Peter, Hans – anything but Standish.

'And Treadwell?'

'From the Home Country, sir,' I said.

What did I know? That's what I'd always been taught to say.

'Your parents are dead?'

Well, I didn't think that was quite right, but I wasn't about to argue.

He pulled a letter out of the file. He rounded on Mr Hellman and started talking in the Mother Tongue.

Roughly translated, it boiled down to the fact that this nice, suburban school in this dead dump of a bombed-out Zone Seven should never had taken me in in the first place. How was it that I had gone so long undetected? I was supposed to be stupid, no good at anything. Though I understood every word they were saying.

'He had been making progress under Miss . . . under his previous teacher . . .' Mr Hellman was beginning to sweat. 'And Treadwell's father was headmaster here before me – his mother a teacher at the school. After Mrs Treadwell . . .'

I waited. They had my full attention. Would he say what happened to my father and mother? Would he? No, because I saw even Mr Hellman wasn't feeling too safe and that watch, when all was said and done, was just made from cheap chrome. No carrots in it like Mr Lush's. I didn't know gold was weighed in carrots. I do now. Whoever dug up gold in the first place must have seen this coming. He knew we would be swapping gold for food.

The leather-coat man asked me again, 'What is special about today?' But slower this time, as if wishing to make a point. Maybe he was thinking I was an idiot and that's the way you speak to idiots.

I knew what was special about that day. Frick-fracking hell, I wouldn't think there was so much as a rat in the occupied territory that didn't know what was special about that day – and no, it was not the spam fritters.

So I said with pride, as if I was driving in an ice-cream-coloured Cadillac, 'It is Thursday, 19th July, 1956, the day the rocket to the moon is launched, and a new era of the history of the Motherland will begin.'

I think I said it quite well for both the headmaster and the leather-coat man's arms shot skywards again. The leather-coat man looked almost misty-eyed behind those skullhole glasses.

'Correct. We will be the first nation in the world to have achieved such a feat, demonstrating our ultimate supremacy.'

The school bell rang as he said it. It was dinner time.

'Have you ever been into the park at the back of your house?'

I was running through all the answers I could give. All lies. And still I was wondering what I was there for.

'No, sir, it is forbidden.'

Twenty

The leather-coat man had X-ray eyes. I was sure of it even though I couldn't see them. They burned right into you. Now I knew what a fish might feel like if the plug was pulled on the sea.

So I floundered and flapped and I said, 'Only once. Or twice.'

The leather-coat man looked at the paper he was holding and said the strangest thing.

'What does the word "eternal" mean?'

Sometimes I think adults are just plain barking mad. Mad. Hairbrush mad.

'It means going on forever, like the great Motherland.'

I put that in like pepper and salt on chips, though I didn't believe it, but frick-fracking hell, what did that matter? I believed in life and one day I was going to the land of Croca-Colas, but these two wise guys didn't need to know that.

'Did you ever see anyone else in the park?'

Too late, I felt the talons sink into me and I realised this was nothing to do with Hector's disappearance, nothing to do with me being unable to spell, or read or write. This was nothing to do with my father being headmaster, or my mother, or even the hens in our back garden – no, this was to do with an altogether more worrying matter.

It was about the moon man.

Twenty-One

Only three weeks ago – three weeks sounded like another century – me and Hector were planning our mission to Planet Juniper. Let the frickwits be thrilled about the moon landings, we knew that our achievement would make a walk on the moon look like a cheap circus trick.

Gramps wasn't bothered one way or another about the moon mission. 'Waste of money,' he said, 'when there are starving people down here on earth.' He belonged to another generation. He'd lived through the wars and not much had got better and a whole lot had got worse. According to Gramps, a man in space wouldn't make a hare's breath of difference. But Hector and I knew better. After all, hadn't we seen the future with our own eyes? Not that we were meant to, but Mr Lush had managed to rig up a television set, and more than just rigged it up, we often received programmes from the land of Croca-Colas. Mr Lush was a bloody wonder.

There was this one programme me and Hector liked best of all. It had a lady in it, all plastic perfect. She shimmered next to this huge fridge in this shiny kitchen. The lady from the television had big lips and cone-shaped boobs. She laughed all the time. This is how I thought the Juniparians would be. On that planet we would be all warm and safe in our own solar system, free from bed bugs and hunger. Bet you that fridge could feed us for a year, no, maybe longer. This woman had a name like a ball – but not like a deflated football. In Croca-Cola Land a ball means a great deal of fun. They were having a ball. We weren't.

This actress was Hector's favourite. The pictures were in black and white but that didn't fool us, not one iota – we knew this promised land was bursting with colour. And that it would all be coming here the minute our rocket landed on Juniper, the minute we'd left our first footprint where no footprint had ever been. I mean, that moment would change everything here. Put an end to the war. It would be an event so humongous in the anus of history that it would become a before and after all of its own making. A 'Were you alive before they discovered Juniper?' event. It would overshadow everything, overshadow the moon landings.

Or so I thought three weeks ago.

Twenty-Two

Hector had been sent to my school, to the same class as me. I was dead chuffed about that. It took Hector less than a week to have Hans Fielder and his merry men under control.

Miss Connolly was our teacher then. She was kind, sat me at the front near her desk, spent time explaining. Miss Connolly didn't like Hans Fielder and his merry gang of frickwits any more than I did. She took a great liking to Hector, though. It turned out he was supernova bright, spoke the home language with only a slight accent, and played the piano, and I don't mean dong-dong merrily on high. He had beautiful hands – long, really thin, long fingers. As for the rest of him he was lanky with a perfect-shaped head, not fish flat at the back. His hair was dark blonde and flopperty thick. I liked the way he swept his hair from his face.

Sadly, Miss Connolly disappeared down a hole in the middle of the autumn term. No explanation. There never is one. Nobody dares ask why. Just there one day and the next disappeared, without leaving a footprint behind to tell us where she had gone. See, I said death and disappearing were the same things. Both stink.

That was when Mr Gunnell appeared. He brought with him no knowledge worth learning. Just propaganda. A minor major man was Mr Gunnell.

On the first day he ordered Hector to have his hair cut to regulation standards. Hector never did. You see Hector was in a league all of his own making. He had sea-green eyes that would go stormy with indifference. Hector had a way of making Mr Gunnell repeat what he had just said so he could take in the hollowness of his words.

It turned out that our new teacher, for all his patriotic fervour for the Motherland, couldn't speak a word of the lingo. That made me smile. He never did understand quite what Hector said. It drove him bonkers knowing Hector had the upper hand.

Twenty-Three

From the start, Mr Gunnell took a dislike to me. My eyes plagued him something rotten. Such an impurity was in itself a good enough reason to have me removed from the school, so he thought. And that was before he realised I couldn't read or write, let alone spell. That little delight came later. As for Hector, he took against him too, simply because he could see right into Mr Gunnell's mouldy old heart.

Our punishment was to be sent to the back of the class. Mr Gunnell thought he was being so clever in ignoring Hector. Except no one could ignore Hector. He was too present, too there, to be ignored. Hector took to standing up to Mr Gunnell. He would say, 'That's wrong, sir, the sum should read . . .'

Mr Gunnell's face would go as red as the word he sat under. One day he could take it no more. He charged at Hector, you could almost hear the engines going in those army-tank arms of his. He lifted his cane, hungry to find the comfort of flesh. The first slash hit Hector's shoulder. He didn't flinch, not once. Neither did he put his hands up to defend himself. He just stood, took the blows, and he stared hard at Mr Gunnell with the hurricane force of his all-seeing green eyes.

That stare took the oil out of Mr Gunnell's arms, I can tell you. He had sweat pouring off him as he turned to walk back down the row of quietly terrified boys. He dropped his cane on the way. Hector, bleeding from the slash he had been given across his face, picked it up and took it to Mr Gunnell's desk. Stupid man, he hadn't seen that coming, had he? No, too busy checking on his toupee tape and wiping the sweat from his brow.

Hector said calmly, 'You forgot this, sir,' and he brought the cane down hard with a crack on Mr Gunnell's pile of exercise books. Mr Gunnell, thinking he was going to be attacked, flinched and put his army-tank arms up over his head.

There's no need to say it, but he never beat Hector again.

Twenty-Four

The day the leather-coat man turned up was one I will never forget. And it had nilch to do with the rocket going to the fricking moon. By then I didn't care any more about the moon landing. Never did in the first place. Why should I? I left that to the likes of Hans Fielder and his merry men. They all swallowed that crappy crap.

Me and Hector instead liked to think about our Planet Juniper. It had three moons, two suns. The folk that lived there were kind, wise and peaceful. They knew who the aliens really were: the Greenflies and the leather-coat men. All of them, Hector said, had come from the red planet Mars. They were Martians here.

I was sure that all we needed to do was get a message to Planet Juniper and they would come and rescue the world, make it possible for me and Hector to live in the land of Croca-Colas. I promised Hector we would. You don't break a promise.

All the brainwashed of the Motherland could get as excited about the moon mission as they liked. I couldn't. Why not? We had the moon man hidden in our cellar.

Twenty-Five

From a window I could see Mr Hellman escorting the leather-coat man back to his black Jag. For a moment Mr Hellman was lost from view in a fog of speeding car fumes.

I had missed school dinner because of having to go to the headmaster's office. I just wish I had missed break time. Break your bone, break your nose, break your soul, break your spirit. Break.

I refuse to be broken.

For some reason Mr Hellman had thought it would be a good idea to put a park bench in the playground. Don't tell me he didn't know exactly what would happen if a bench was pushed diagonally across the corner of the playground. I mean, you didn't have to be good at maths to work that out. The sheep sat on the wooden back of the bench so no teacher could see what was going on. Then, in the tiny triangle behind the bench, a boy beat up a weaker one, a runt, or one that didn't fit in, one who stood out from the flock.

Hans Fielder was his old self now there was no more Hector to cramp his style. He was the drawing pin. He sent his merry men to round me up and push me behind the bench.

'What would a officer want with a dunce?'

'You mean the leather-coat man?' I said. I saw that Hans Fielder was wound up tighter than a clockwork soldier, ready to do battle.

'Of course I mean him, you fricking moron.'

You see, Hans Fielder had from birth greedily drunk all this Motherland sheep milk. Mrs Fielder has eight, nine, ten, eleven children. Can't remember, not good at counting sheep. What I know is that she and her husband survive on their rewards for the patriotic support of the Motherland. They take pride in their work, which is to report on all the good citizens who don't toe the party line. Yes, these Fielders have well-fed, well-clothed children.

It's easy to spot the parents who are collaborators in

our school. Their sons wear long trousers. I, like most of the underclass, wear shorts that once were trousers before I grew too long for them. Now they are cut off below the knee, the two drain pipes of fabric kept in my mother's sewing box in case repairs are necessary.

Hans Fielder, of the long trousers and the new school blazer, pushed me up hard against the playground wall and asked the question again. His sidekicks all gathered round.

I didn't fight back when they started in on me again.

Gramps once said, 'Whatever else you do, Standish, don't raise your fists. Turn away. If they throw you out of that school, well . . .'

He never finished what he was saying. There was no need.

But I couldn't keep quiet any longer.

I said, 'The next time I see the leather-coat man I might tell him all about your mother.'

Hans Fielder stopped punching me.

'What about my mother?' he asked.

'How she informs on people, makes up lies, sends innocent people to the maggot farms – to keep you in new trousers.'

That stopped him. Doubt is a great worm in a crispy, red apple. You didn't need to be a rocket scientist to know who the real idiots were here: Hans Fielder who believed he was destined for greatness, along with his merry gang. They were all bleating sheep, the whole maladjusted lot of them. They never questioned anything. There was not one of a rare breed of Whys among them, just plain, shorn, bleached sheep. The brain-branded idiots couldn't see that, like all the rest of us who lived in Zone Seven, they were never going anywhere. The only chance Hans Fielder had of escape was to be sent to fight the Obstructors, and that was as good as booking yourself a slot in the crematorium. But that realisation had yet to dawn on him.

So the beating continued. I thought of my flesh as a wall. The me inside the wall they can't bully, they can't touch, so while they beat the drum of my skin I thought hard about that leather-coat man and where his black Jag was going next. In my mind's eye I could see it arriving in our road. He wasn't going to have any problems finding where we live. After all, it was the only row of houses left standing. I saw the leather-coat man finding our hens, the TV, pushing Gramps down to the cellar, and, worst of all, discovering the moon man. I was seeing this all in my head like a film being played and ending badly.

'Standish Treadwell,' shouted Mr Gunnell, 'what are you doing behind there? The bell has gone.'

I hadn't even noticed it. I tasted the blood in my mouth, felt my nose and thought, at least it isn't broken.

Twenty-Six

'Standish Treadwell!' Mr Gunnell shouted again, his face red. His eyes bulged out of his head as did two veins leading up to that troublesome toupee.

I climbed out from behind the bench and stood in front of Mr Gunnell. I had a bloody nose and a half-shut eye that refused to open. He was holding his cane, tap-tap-tapping it on the palm of his hand, and his tongue was sticking out sideways from his small mean mouth. It was then that I had a revelation of sorts. I was taller than he was. I could see his tank arms were well oiled for a beating. I could see that like it or not he was forced to look up at me. Just as he had to look up at Hector.

'You can't keep hitting me,' I said. 'I'm taller than you. Pick on someone your own size.'

The whole class was watching, awestruck. Since Hector, no one, and I mean, no one, not even the Head Perfect, talked back to a teacher. The wheels of Mr Gunnell's mind were visibly turning.

'Treadwell, your shoelaces are undone.'

I bent down, ducking the fists, feeling the cane on my back. I glanced up quickly, saw his chin jutting out and without a second thought, I stood to attention fast, making sure I hit him as hard as I could under the jaw. I heard with pleasure the sound of his teeth clacking together then pushed my hand out in a salute, as hard as it could go, straight into his chest. I must say, even I was suprised by my own strength. Mr Gunnell tripped backwards and his toupee, a dead rabbit, came free from its trap and jumped unceremoniously on to the tarmac.

The entire class started to laugh, including Hans Fielder, but it was Little Eric, he of the short trousers, of the bleach-bowl bright hair, who was laughing the hardest. He couldn't stop himself, especially when Mr Gunnell took another step backwards and accidentally stamped on his toupee.

Twenty-Seven

I was thinking this is no laughing matter and now Mr Gunnell will do me in. His eyes were glazed over with a look of pure hatred. He came towards me, cane lifted. I waited for the blow but at the last minute he had a change of plan. You see, Little Eric was still laughing. He pulled the boy towards him by his ear then he started to beat him, first with the cane until it broke, then with his fists. He didn't stop, his punches coming harder and faster. Little Eric was on the ground, curled into a ball, crying for his mummy.

This seemed to fuel the rage in Mr Gunnell for he was now kicking, kicking the shit out of Little Eric, screaming, 'Don't you ever laugh at me again . . . I am to be treated with respect!'

The more Little Eric wept, the harder Mr Gunnell went at him. We all watched paralysed as gobbets of blood splashed on the tarmac. Eric Owen wasn't moving and I knew exactly what Mr Gunnell was about to do as he lifted his army boot high above Little Eric's head.

I rushed at Mr Gunnell and I hit that frick-fracking bastard as hard as I could. His boot narrowly missed smashing Little Eric's brains in. To make doubly sure Mr Gunnell could do no more harm, I hit him again hard on his nose. I heard it crack and he yelped in pain, bloody mucus rolling into his moustache.

Miss Phillips had been sent by Mr Hellman to find out what was keeping us. We were the only class not in the assembly hall and in five minutes history would be made: the rocket would be launched from the Motherland. At first Miss Phillips couldn't properly see what had happened because all the boys were gathered round Eric Owen.

'Mr Gunnell,' she snapped, 'what is going on?'

'A matter of discipline, that is all,' replied Mr Gunnell.

Twenty-Eight

Miss Phillips pushed her way through the terrified pupils and saw Little Eric Owen lying there like a twisted sack, his hair no longer bleach blond but blood red, his face raw mutton, one of his eyes hanging out of its socket.

Mr Gunnell was standing upright. Everyone was silent. We watched Miss Phillips bend down over what was left of Eric Owen. She lifted his floppy broken arm, hoping to find a pulse. She turned to one of the sheep.

'Go and get help – quickly.' The boy ran off. 'Who did this?' she asked, shaking with anger. 'Who is the monster that did this?'

'Standish Treadwell,' said Mr Gunnell.

She looked at me. 'What has happened here, Standish?' And I told her.

'Did you do this, Mr Gunnell?' she said, her voice incredulous.

'I won't be laughed at,' said Mr Gunnell, patting his non-existent toupee with a bloody hand. 'I demand respect. I am no one's laughing stock.'

Now Mr Hellman was running towards us, followed by other members of the staff. Miss Phillips closed Little Eric's one good eye and gently pushed the other back into its socket. She stood up slowly. There was blood on her skirt. There was blood everywhere.

'I have called for an ambulance. Difficult at this time,' said Mr Hellman, not daring to look down.

Miss Phillips took a deep breath through that snub nose of hers and said, very calmly, 'Mr Hellman, the boy is dead.'

'He's just play-acting,' said Mr Gunnell. 'He will be all right.'

'No, he won't,' said Miss Phillips.

'This is Standish Treadwell's doing,' said Mr Gunnell.

I said nothing.

Mr Hellman looked at me as if I was a creature from out of space.

Still, I said nothing.

To my surprise, it was Hans Fielder, Mr Gunnell's pet sheep, who said loud and clear, 'Standish Treadwell had nothing to do with this, sir. He tried to save Little Eric. It was Mr Gunnell who beat him to death.'

'Liar!' shouted Mr Gunnell. 'You fucking little sod of a liar!'

Hans Fielder stood tall, looked straight at his teacher, his hair golden blonde, his eyes, cheap plastic-bag blue, shining with a passion.

'I never lie, sir,' he said. 'Never.'

Twenty-Nine

All I wanted to do was go home and make sure Gramps was all right. I knew well enough if I were to make a run for it, me, Gramps, plus the moon man, would end up in a maggot farm. Once you're there you're nothing but fly fodder.

The whole school was gathered in the gymnasium for this momentous occasion. The place smelled of over-boiled cabbage, cigarettes and corruption. The teachers had on their glad drags. Pathetic, the whole fricking lot of them.

In that silence I wanted to scream at the top of my voice: why is there no wolf among you to protect us? Teacher. Please note that word: teacher. You are supposed to teach, not beat your pupils' fricking brains out.

Thirty

Bad news spreads fast, doesn't need words. Even those who didn't know Little Eric Owen knew he was dead.

It was the school caretaker who had covered him in a dust sheet. They left his broken body lying abandoned in the playground. No one was allowed to miss this hiatus hernia of a historical day when the pitiless pure of the inhuman race sent a man to the moon.

Thirty-One

A huge flag of the Motherland smothered the back wall of the gym. There, on a makeshift stand, sat a make-do television. For this great event, every school in the whole of the occupied territory had been lent one working television for the day.

Mr Muller, the maths teacher, tried his best to make the fuzz go away. He held the aerial at different heights, his arms wildly thrashing.

'There, just there,' shouted Mr Hellman.

'I can't stay like this with my arms up, it's preposterous!' Mr Muller spat the words into his wirehair, flea-ridden moustache.

A hat stand was utilised. A very technical way of solving the problem in this age of moon men and murders.

The TV still didn't quite work. The images splintered, came and went.

'Can you all see?' asked Mr Muller.

No one said a word. They had seen too much already.

Thirty-Two

Hector and me – or should that be Hector and I? – used to do puppet shows. We made a theatre out of an old box. I think Mr Muller might have been better off doing a puppet show than trying to conjure a picture from that broken thing. It could have been presented quite well. All he would have needed was one wobbly rocket pulled on a wire towards a wobbly moon where tin foil astronauts walked on a surface made of wobbly cheese.

You know, I didn't care a blue parrot's tutu if we saw this moment in history or not. I think that maybe – no, not maybe, there's no maybe about it – I think the Greenflies and the leather-coat men, or Martians as Hector used to call them, shouldn't be going anywhere except back to their frick-fracking planet. I don't buy all this pure race chatty crap. There's nothing pure about any one of those frickwits.

It was kind of the President of the Motherland to address us. The leader of the moronic Martians. She always looked the same, never changed. Her hair a construction of steel wire, her eyes unblinking. She didn't fool me, not one iota. Underneath that proganda-perfect face paint she had red scaly skin and a hole for a mouth. Her words were worms that buried themselves into your worried mind, to rot all thoughts of freedom.

'Today, we, the race of purity, will demonstrate our technical supremacy over the corrupt countries whose ambition is to destroy the great Motherland.'

She made her usual non-stopping Olympic speech, at the end of which we all stood to attention, rows of nutcracker would-be soldiers. We saluted. I noticed it was the weakest Motherland salute I had ever seen this school give. Only Mr Gunnell's arm was out rod-stiff, his gobstopper eyes glazed.

We sat down cross-legged on the floor again. Amazingly the picture became clear and we were shown photographs of each of the three astronauts. Their names flashed up on the screen. Names that were supposed to be hard to forget. Names that I couldn't remember. To me they were one long, unreadable word that joined a whole bunch of other unreadable words.

They appeared on each of the group photos that had been plastered round Zone Seven: ARO5 SOL3 ELD9. Only after the moon man arrived had I looked again at that word. Some of the letters were printed on his space suit. And here were the letters again on the television. Each astronaut's photograph given a part of that meaningless word.

ARO5 – clean cut with a short, bristled head of hair. Next to him, as always, was SOL3. He looked as if his face had been polished white, so that it shone. I knew he was the Mothers for Purity's golden hero. The last of the trio was ELD9. His head was shaven, his face well fed, pumped up, pumped out. But I knew what he really looked like.

ELD9 was what was printed on the space suit of the moon man. ELD9 wasn't in the Motherland. He was in our cellar.

Thirty-Three

The camera turned its attention to the control room. Up to that point I had thought there might be a way out of all this stinking shit. Then I knew that there wasn't. The control room was full of men in uniforms and white coats. I wanted to get up, throw caution to the mangle. I was stretched out good and proper anyway. I stood and walked to the very front. You see, I was certain that in among all those scientists I spied Mr Lush. Wait – hold it – don't change that picture.

Frick-fracking hell, I was right. Lead stones in my shoes. Lead stones in my head. Lead stones in my heart. I knew then what the secret was, the secret that Hector had refused to tell me. That the moon man was unable to say.

Thirty-Four

The rocket was launched into a pale grey sky. Of course, we only saw this in black and white, it was the commentator who was doing the colouring in by numbers. The rocket was red, the sky was blue. It all looked pretty grey to me. Higher and higher it went until it was just a dot.

There was a commotion outside the gym. The leather-coat man had returned, accompanied by an impressive array of Greenflies and detectives. The detectives were wearing square-framed sunglasses. I suppose they made it harder to see the evidence. The leather-coat man snapped one of his leather-gloved fingers and the Greenflies marched into the gym. One of them turned off the television and Mr Gunnell was ushered outside.

Mr Hellman ordered us back to our classrooms. Hans Fielder, Head Perfect, was put in charge of our class.

I was sitting next to the window, no longer daydreaming. There was too much reality, it shut out all daydreams. I could see the paint-spattered white dust sheet that lay over Little Eric's body. It was stained red. A halo of flies hovered above him.

Hans Fielder looked decidedly uncomfortable. He was seated in Mr Gunnell's chair. No one was speaking. Finally, a detective pushed the door half open and shouted out two names.

I knew this was coming and so did Hans Fielder. We followed the detective down the stairs to the bench outside Mr Hellman's office. Bet you two matching socks and one pair of long trousers that Hans Fielder had never had to sit there before. I had a feeling this was my last time. I hated to think what would happen to me and Gramps if they'd found the moon man in our cellar.

Hans Fielder was called in. He rose from that bench like a flying saucer. The door closed behind him and one of the Greenflies, rifle across his chest, stood guard over the door. Or over me. I'm not sure which.

I heard talking, then Mr Hellman's cane. Hans Fielder

was spat back into the corridor. He had pissed his pants. Nearly everyone did after Mr Hellman's beatings. Bet that one was harder than his average. He had to impress the leather-coat man. Bet that was his only hope of clinging on to that cheap watch of his.

Then it was my turn.

Thirty-Five

The leather-coat man was seated in Mr Hellman's chair. Mr Hellman was standing upright rubbing his wrist. His black hair dye ran down the back of his neck in dribbles of sweat.

'We meet again, Standish Treadwell,' said the leather-coat man.

I nodded. He had removed one of his gloves. His bare hand was large, deadfish white. Before him on the desk was Mr Hellman's watch.

'I didn't notice it before,' he said. 'You have different-coloured eyes: one blue and the other, a light brown.'

Was he being poetic or just stating the obvious? That I had two definite defects?

I kept quiet.

'Am I right in saying,' asked the leather-coat man, 'that you were beaten up because you wouldn't tell the other boys about our interview?'

I answered that one. 'Yes, sir.'

'Why?'

'Because it's no one's business but my own.'

The leather-coat man was studying me very carefully indeed.

I put on my best vacant face. If you are clever, know more than you should, you stand out like a green sky above a blue field, and, as we all know, the President of the Motherland believes that artists who do those sorts of paintings should be sterilised.

I was waiting to be caned or taken away.

'Standish Treadwell,' said the leather-coat man, 'I don't think for one moment you are as stupid as you would like us to believe.'

My lips were sealed.

'There is a lot going on in that head of yours,' he said. 'Do you know "stupid" is what Mother Nature intended all mere mortals to be? Stupid rises to the surface like shit and cream. Stupid means everyone does as they are told. Stupid wouldn't break his teacher's nose, even if that teacher was in the process of killing a fellow pupil. Stupid would stand and stare. You're not stupid, Standish Treadwell, are you?'

The leather-coat man suddenly brought his bare fist down hard on Mr Hellman's watch. It shattered with a satisfying ping as small wheels of time spun across the desk.

Mr Hellman was shaking.

'I am waiting,' said the leather-coat man, as with one sweep of his hand the crumbs of time vanished into the waste-paper bin.

I said, 'I think a wise man would have turned a blind eye.'

'Which eye, Treadwell, the blue or the brown?' He laughed, a rattatat of a laugh, then turned to Mr Hellman. 'What do you say? he asked, the smile still on his face.

'I say,' said Mr Hellman, through steel-welded teeth, 'I say that Standish Treadwell is expelled from this school.'

'A pity that you didn't think to do that a long time ago,' said the leather-coat man.

Thirty-Six

I didn't know what I was expected to do after that. So I walked unaccompanied back to my classroom, certain it was a trap of some sort. On the first floor landing I stopped and looked out of the window at the playground. The leather-coat man was walking with Mr Gunnell past the body of Little Eric. He stopped and Mr Gunnell looked suprised. The leather-coat man calmly took his pistol from his holster and placed the barrel against Mr Gunnell's temple. One shot rung out, ricocheting round the playground. Mr Gunnell slumped to the ground.

Do you know? I didn't give a shit.

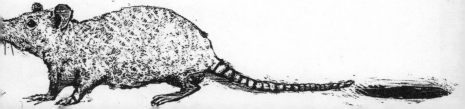

Thirty-Seven

In the classroom Hans Fielder was standing in the dunce's corner with a pair of scissors. He had Robinson Crusoed his trousers. Goodness knows how many lies Mrs Fielder had to make up to be rewarded with those. I don't think she is going to be too delighted to see she has a rebel on her hands. But that's her problem, not mine. No, my problem is elephantine. How do you eat an elephant, sir? Bit by tiny bit.

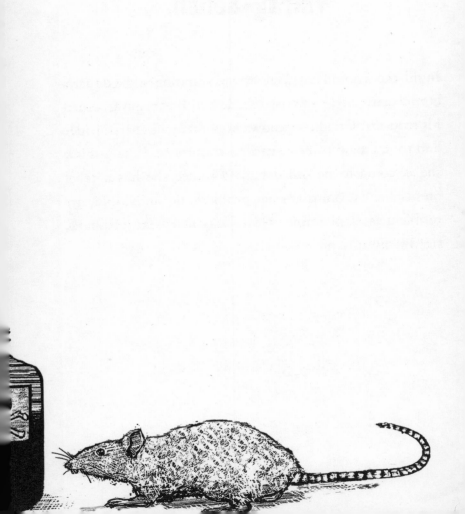

Thirty-Eight

I told the Greenfly who was in charge of us that I had been expelled. He said nothing. I don't think they cover what to do with uncooperative pupils in their manual. Every boy in the class had his head down. I was an undesirable among the sheep. I returned to my desk. I felt stupid and didn't know what to do, so I lifted the lid. There was a note pinned inside. It was written in big words so that I, who can't read, could read it.

YOU AND YOUR GRANDFATHER
ARE IN GRAVE DANGER.
TONIGHT THE OBSTRUCTORS
WILL COME FOR THE VISITOR.

I got the gist of it. I put the piece of paper in my shorts pocket. There was nothing else in my desk. From the classroom window I saw a van drive into the playground. Two orderlies, overseen by the Greenflies, gently picked up Little Eric Owen's body and less gently, Mr Gunnell's, and placed them in the van.

What that note told me was that this time there was no get out of jail card.

I was in the corridor when I saw Miss Phillips. She was still wearing that blood-soaked skirt. She walked right past me without a word and I nearly jumped out of myself when I felt a finger on my shoulder. Miss Phillips had darted back while the clockwork camera was turned the other way.

She whispered in my ear, 'Tell Harry they know,' then ran to the point in the corridor where the camera would next find her.

I kept my face as dumb as possible which, considering what Miss Phillips had just said, wasn't easy.

Thirty-Nine

There was blood on the tarmac. One of Little Eric's shoes, scuffed and worn, lay there abandoned. The sole of that shoe hollered, megaphone loud.

'Standish, wake up, you fricking, daydreaming bastard! Wake up! Wake up or you'll be dead like me.'

In the guardhouse the school caretaker didn't even look up from his paper. I was about to tell him I had been expelled when he pressed the button that electrically opened the school gates. I walked, snail-slow out of the school, wondering why no one stopped me.

Forty

Did you think I hadn't seen cruelty like that before? We all had. Nothing like the unexpected, terrifying death to keep everyone calm and orderly.

I was doing my best to imitate my old self, the one that looked as if he was lost in a dream. My plan was simple: go home.

'Standish!'

Coming down the road towards me was Gramps. We tried never to run, as that drew attention, and what both Gramps and me wanted most in Zone Seven was no attention whatsoever.

When I reached him, I said, 'Where were you?'

'In the old church, watching the TV.'

Only then did it strike me, lightning-bolt hard, that

someone must have ordered Gramps to come and fetch me.

'They said there had been some trouble at school.'

'Yes. Mr Gunnell killed Little Eric Owen and I've been expelled.'

He put his hand on my shoulder and squeezed it. That squeeze said everything. It said, thank God you are all right.

We carried on walking, intentionally slowly, up the street where once there were shops that sold things you might have wanted. Not now. All the shops were boarded up.

Half under my breath and in the quietest of whispers, so Gramps had to lean towards me, I said, 'This is a trap.'

'I know,' replied Gramps.

No matter how bad things looked, Gramps had always seemed a giant to me. He wasn't made up of any monstrous parts.

Forty-One

There were two men, plain-clothes policemen, following us in a car.

Gramps smiled at me like it was a good summer afternoon, a day to be proud of.

'Did you hear the President of the Motherland speak?' he asked.

'Yes,' I said. 'No, not really. The TV set . . .'

One of the men in the car had a pair of binoculars. He was lip-reading.

I said, 'Did you see the astronauts walking out to the rocket? Cripes, they are so brave.'

'Very impressive,' replied Gramps. 'Good to know about all the missiles they can launch from the moon. That will do it, put an end to the enemies of the Motherland.'

'We missed that bit,' I said. 'It must have happened while Mr Gunnell was being shot.'

Either we were just too boring for the detectives to bother with any longer, or they'd found something more important to do, for their car sped off.

We carried on, past the disused bus shelter at the roundabout and crossed the deserted road. It was then I told him about Little Eric, and about the note and Miss Phillips. He listened carefully, weighed it all up.

At one end of our road were the grand, rooster-breasted houses. Those were where the good Families for Purity lived. They looked smart enough, but they were only stuck together with the glue of dead men's bones.

In the distance, at the very top of the road, you could see that hideous building which should have been left in ashes when it first burned down. I suppose it added to the stage effect that all was as it should be. But I'll tell you this for nothing – it wasn't.

That huge ugly building was lit up. It shone brighter than the stars, even in the daytime. That was something. People in Zone Seven dared not ask why. We just wondered what was going on inside. Why did it need so much electricity when we were lucky to get an hour or two a day? You could hear the citizens of Zone Seven silently ask that question. It crept along the streets, oozed out of everyone you met.

I wished I didn't have even a hint of what the answer might be, but I did.

Forty-Two

Down the dip in the road where the tall trees hid the rest of our street, the houses were just rubble, destroyed for harbouring terrorist cells or undesirables.

That summer, in the wilderness of crumbling bricks and mortar, white roses had appeared in those derelict suburbs. Gramps said that if man was mad enough to destroy itself, at least the rats and cockroaches would have front-row seats, be able to enjoy the sight of Mother Nature reclaiming the earth.

Outside our house two black cars were waiting. We watched as the television set was carried away.

'What if they find him?' I asked in a whisper.

'They won't, not even with their dogs. Neither will they find the hens.'

'So why did you let them have the TV?'

I knew that was the end of of the plastic lady who had a ball of a time in the land of Croca-Colas.

'Because if I didn't, they would be even more suspicious that we are up to no good. Forfeiting the television is a lighter penalty than the alternative.'

It was not much comfort.

Forty-Three

It was on my birthday in March, after the terrible winter, that Gramps had given me his present.

So much had changed since Hector arrived eight months earlier that I'd forgotten all about the football. Gramps had mended it and gift-wrapped it in old newspaper.

'Can we kick it, or do we just look at it?' Hector had asked.

'You could play for the Home Country with that ball,' said Gramps.

Mrs Lush had spent weeks collecting all she needed to make my birthday cake. She told us that the secret ingredients in the cake were her recipes. She had swapped them for butter, for sugar. Mrs Lush was a whizz at making meals from thin air. Anyone who could do that had something worth swapping.

I thought it was the best birthday tea I could remember. I tried to forget about my mum and dad. It hurt too much to think about them. Except they kept breaking through the sound barrier of my daydreams.

When my parents had been teachers at my school, Dad managed to at least look as if he toed the party line. Mum didn't. She made it as clear as glass that she had no intention of teaching a whole load of rubbish to children who deserved better. The Mothers for Purity hated her. She wouldn't treat their long-trousered sons any different from those with short trousers.

One day, out of the blue, the Greenflies came to our house and dragged my mum away. She clutched at the kitchen table but only managed to grab the cloth. Everything crashed to the floor. Gramps had to hold Dad down, using all his strength, otherwise we would all have been maggot meat. I had never seen my dad cry before. I can't remember what I did. Maybe I wasn't there. The next day, Mum was driven home.

I rushed up to her. The look in her eyes told me that she didn't know who I was. Blood ran down the sides of her mouth. She said nothing, not one word, not even when she was seated at the kitchen table. Dad went on his knees and finally he made her open her mouth. Gramps put his hands over my eyes and took me out of the room.

That night, Dad came and told me they had to go, that I was to stay with Gramps. He and Mum would be back for us, he promised.

I am still waiting.

Forty-Four

Gramps and Hector's parents had made a huge vegetable plot in our adjoining gardens. It was hoped that it would supply us with most of the food we needed for the coming winter. We'd even taken over a third garden, which was a bit useless for growing things, but had a small potting shed.

The vegetable garden meant there was nowhere we could play football. The road was out of bounds because of the four o'clock curfew. So that left the park on the other side of the wall. We knew we weren't allowed to go there, it was expressly forbidden. I told Hector about how I had found the flattened football in the first place. How I hadn't seen any Greenflies there. The trouble was that once we had that football the temptation was too great. It was so

easy. We went through the air raid shelter tunnel to reach the park beyond. Cautious as hen's teeth we were to begin with, then, when we knew there were no Greenflies, knew that Gramps and Mr and Mrs Lush hadn't clocked what we were up to, we went as many times as we could.

It was only when the wall that ran along the bottom of our garden started to grow that we decided it was best to leave it for the time being. At least until the wall stopped growing. But that wall just kept getting taller. It didn't make any sense to us. The wall was already neck-breaking high to begin with. Why did anyone feel the need to make it higher?

We heard Gramps and Mr and Mrs Lush say, 'It's going to start again.'

Neither Hector or I knew what they meant.

'What will start again?' I asked Mr Lush as we ate our tea.

Mr and Mrs Lush both looked to Gramps for an answer. Gramps wasn't a man to waste words, so he said nothing.

Soon that wall was nearly as high as our house, if not higher. It began to cast a long shadow over the vegetable garden, cutting out the sunlight. It cast a long shadow over everybody in Zone Seven.

Forty-Five

One day, eight or nine weeks before the moon mission, Hector and I started playing football on the crazy paving, near the wall by the potting shed. We were in the middle of a really good game when I went and kicked the ball right up into the sky. It was a freak accident, it wasn't meant to go that high. The ball flew right over that frick-fracking wall. We stood there open-mouthed, unable to believe what I'd done.

'Doesn't matter,' Hector said, 'I'll nip through the tunnel and find it.'

'No,' I said, 'it's too dangerous. The ball's gone, forget it.'

The trouble was, Hector couldn't.

Forty-Six

It rained every day after we lost the football so neither the Lushes nor Gramps realised it had gone missing.

Hector and I concentrated on building our rocket in the attic. The newspapers were full of the moon mission. Note the word 'newspapers'. That was the first time I had ever seen one. Propaganda rags, as Gramps called them. Hector read them to me. It was always the same rubbish. Always about the great Motherland, about the purity of the astronauts who were going to conquer space. In the end we decided the paper was better without the words. The pictures were good, though. We kept those and made papier mâché from the rest.

'If we are to go into space, Standish,' Hector said, 'we wouldn't want to go to the moon with this lot there.'

I found Planet Juniper myself. I found it in my head but that didn't matter. Hector thought it was probably the best discovery I had ever come up with.

I drew the planet. I drew the Juniparians. I drew the rocket, more like a flying saucer than something that pricked the sky. Hector decided we should build it in the attic. Both of us started to collect all the things we might need. It wasn't that easy making a spacecraft out of nothing, not when everything was used, reused and reused again. The idea that there was rubbish was a joke.

But that week, the week I kicked the football over the wall, the week it rained, Mrs Lush had given us an old ironing-board cover. There was no electricity so there was no point in ironing. A waste of time, a waste of hope. Tell you this for nothing, that ironing-board cover stopped me worrying about us being fried or frozen in space.

Once I had heard Mr Lush say, 'If they believe they can make it through all the radiation that's round the moon in no more than silver foil, they are fools.'

Now we had the ironing-board cover I reckoned we had nothing to worry about.

I asked Mr Lush if he knew how far away the moon was from earth.

'Roughly,' he said, '221,463 miles.'

A bloody walking cyclops, was Mr Lush.

The flying saucer was nearly ready when Hector became ill.

Forty-Seven

Mrs Lush was a doctor but there was little she could do for Hector except nurse him. She said a doctor with no medicine is the same as a pianist with no piano.

Gramps tried to conjure up some aspirin. No easy task. After all, we were the only people who were left on our road and you couldn't just go up to one of the double rooster-breasted houses and ask for their help. Gramps told us it would be the quickest way to become oven-roasted meat.

It was when Hector's fever was high that the Greenflies rounded up every able-bodied person in Zone Seven. They left Hector. He was too sick to stand upright. They wouldn't allow Mrs Lush to stay with him either. We were taken to the park in front of the hideous building at the top of our road. Mrs Fielder and her Mothers for Purity were ordered to attend. I thought that was a good sign.

Mr Lush said gloomily, 'There are no good signs in Zone Seven.'

We all stood, hundreds of us, bunched together. I saw Miss Phillips in the crowd. She edged her way closer towards us until she was standing beside Gramps. The Greenflies were pushing us around with the butts of their guns, pulling out the well-fed, long-trousered brigade, making them stand at the front. On a podium before us were several men with cameras. We waited.

A humdinger of a car came up the road, stopped, and out stepped a man in a mac with a very bad haircut. What he was doing there I hadn't a snowflake of an idea. He stood and said nothing while a leather-coat man shouted into a megaphone. He asked all those who spoke the barber's language to put up their hands. To my amazement everyone did except Gramps, me and the Lushes. We kept our hands down. The cameras flashed, the bulbs popped. I had never heard of the barber's language before. I thought it must be to do with a bad haircut. That's why I didn't put my hand up. Gramps didn't put his hand up because he knew it was a trick to make it look as if we were all saluting the Motherland, and we weren't.

Mrs Lush was so pleased to find that Hector had slept the whole time she had been away. More to the point, Gramps had managed to get a bottle of aspirin.

Hector smiled weakly when I told him about being asked if we spoke the barber's language.

'I wondered,' I said, 'if it had anything to do with the man in the mac and his bad haircut.'

'Standish,' said Hector, 'he is our Commander-in-Chief.'

'You mean that man with the bad haircut is in charge of these shorn shores of ours?'

Hector had closed his eyes and I thought he might be asleep when he started to laugh.

'Only you, Standish. Only you.'

Forty-Eight

Every day I went to school and every day I came home hoping Hector would be better. Then the fever broke and Mrs Lush said that he had finally turned the corner.

I didn't know there were corners in illness.

The weather too changed. It stopped raining. Hector was allowed out of bed as long as he took it easy. Hector never took anything easy. It wasn't Hector's way. By this time the flying saucer was all but finished. We had collected all the newpapers we could find and given the spacecraft a protective coat of papier mâché. It fitted the two of us and we sat on cushions in the middle with a control panel made out of old tops and cans.

I tell you, I believed with every part of me that in the next week or so Hector and me would be out of there on our own mission to Planet Juniper.

Forty-Nine

Hector was distant. I asked what the matter was and he said nothing. Maybe the illness had taken more out of him than I thought. But I had never seen him like this. I wondered what I had done wrong.

As we walked home on his first day back at school, he said, 'Standish, you should ignore bullies. Don't play their games. That's what the creeps want you to do.'

'I don't,' I said. 'Anyway, it's OK now you're back.'

He was silent a long time.

Then he said, 'Don't count on it.'

Fifty

That afternoon we all sat down for tea. It was a bright evening, and kicking a ball around wouldn't have gone amiss.

Gramps was bringing some boiled potatoes to the table when he asked, 'Where's the football? I haven't seen it for a while.'

I was about to say that we – or rather I – had kicked it over the wall when Hector said, 'I'll get it.'

I stopped eating. Suddenly I wasn't hungry. Not after Hector came in with the red football, for I knew it meant he had been through the air raid shelter tunnel and had seen what was on the other side of that wall.

Mrs Lush and Gramps seemed to be unaware of what Hector had done. Only Mr Lush looked like he knew.

Fifty-One

That night when the lights were out I asked Hector what was on the other side of the wall.

Hector said, 'Go to sleep.'

'I can't,' I said. 'You are keeping something from me.'

Hector sat up in bed. The walls of the house were thin. He put his finger to his mouth. I could see him clearly due to the moon that spilled its light on to the bare floorboards of our room.

We carefully made our way to the attic. One candle in a jar was all the light we had. That and the moon, of course.

When we were in the attic with the ladder pulled up, I said, 'What's behind the wall?'

'Nothing.'

'That's a lie. Why are you lying to me?'

'Look,' said Hector, 'I got the ball back. That's enough, isn't it?'

'No. Tell me what you saw.'

'I can't.'

'Why not?'

'Because. Because I promised I would keep it secret.'

'Who did you promise?'

'My father,' said Hector. 'I can't break that promise.'

I was so cross with him. My feet were frozen and I thought, frick-frack this, I'm off to bed.

'Standish,' said Hector as I got to the trap door, 'don't you want to launch the spacecraft?'

I looked at that papier mâché rocket and said, 'You think it's only a game. You don't believe there is a Planet Juniper. You just think I made it up –'

'No, Standish, I do believe,' Hector interrupted. 'I believe the best thing we have is our imagination and you have that in bucketloads.'

We sat in our cardboard flying saucer with its ironing-board cover. Slashes of moonlight shone through the holes in the roof.

'Once we had a tall house in the city of Tyker,' Hector

said quietly. 'We had servants to cook and clean. Everything smelled of polish and money. It was all taken away from us and we ended up in Zone Seven.'

'Why?'

'Because of what my father did.'

'What did he do?'

Hector was silent, then he said, 'Best you don't know.'

I said that we should launch the spacecraft while there was still time. I don't know why it came to me, but it did. I saw Hector as someone on the verge of a long journey. The thought that he might go alone was unbearable.

Fifty-Two

I woke with a sore head, my eyelids thick and heavy. I remembered that Hector and I had curled up together inside the spacecraft, imagining we saw the stars pass us by. We were on our way to Juniper when sleep overtook us. Bit by conscious bit I knew something was very wrong. I was lying on the same blanket but in an empty attic. No flying saucer. No Hector.

I went down to the kitchen. Gramps was sitting at the table, his head in his hands.

'Where's Hector?' I asked.

Gramps said not a word. I went into every room to look for him. I couldn't find Mr and Mrs Lush either. Finally, I went back to the kitchen. Gramps stood there by the teapot.

'Where is Hector? I shouted.

Gramps put his finger to his mouth. He pointed to a piece of paper on the table. It had writing on it. His handwriting. I knew what it said. I didn't need the written words to tell me. I knew they had been taken.

I felt the scream rise. Gramps caught hold of me and we toppled to the floor. We were both crying. Gramps held his hand firmly over my mouth.

I still have that scream in me.

Fifty-Three

Gramps pulled me to my feet. Still his hand was over my mouth. Still I could feel the scream in me. He took me outside. We stood next to the vegetable plot in the rain.

'I think the house is bugged,' was all he said.

'Why didn't they take us too? Why?' I shouted through his fingers. The words returned to me warm, fired up with rage. There was a lump in my throat so solid it almost suffocated me.

'I don't know,' replied Gramps. 'Do you?'

'No. Yes. There was a secret. But what it was, Hector wouldn't tell me.'

'Good,' said Gramps. 'I'll take you to school.'

'No. No, never. I am never –'

'You have to, Standish. You just have to.' He let go of me. There was nothing then to keep me standing. Nothing. Gramps' words trailed behind him, hot air from a leaden balloon. At the back door he said, 'Do it for Hector.'

I was soaked by the time I went back into the house. Gramps had the radio on, tuned to the only station that the authorities allowed us mere lava mites to listen to. Dripple for the workers of the Motherland. They sang it loud, they sang it clear.

And once those feet did tread upon silver sand
And footprints deep marked out new moons of
    Motherland
Which all salute with upraised hand.

I went upstairs and put on my school uniform. Every part of me dead. Limp. Dead.

Fifty-Four

In the kitchen Gramps had made tea. He had broken into the bank, he'd put a fresh spoonful of tea in the infuser. That's something we didn't do often. Splash out, why not? After all they have taken your best friend, your brother. We sat at the kitchen table, drank our tea in silence.

Fifty-Five

What can I say about the days after Hector was taken? You see, once you are rubbed out you never existed. Night, day, day, night. All blue. Couldn't sleep. Couldn't eat. Went to school where no one talked to me. No one asked about Hector. Because they daren't. His name was erased from the register. He was expendable. That was the disease he was born with. Weren't we all, in the Motherland? Except Mr Gunnell. He had the foolish notion that he was exceptional. The frickwit.

Hans Fielder, the leader of the torture lounge, had left me, the untouchable, alone. Until, that is, the visit from the leather-coat man.

Fifty-Six

What I remember about Gramps after the Lushes went was that he looked older, more worried, with each day that passed. We were being watched. One thing bled into another. The wound kept oozing grief, no matter how many bandages of 'it will be all right'.

In the evenings we listened to the radio. Gramps took to writing down what he wanted to say. Half pictures, half words. Only in our minds were we free to dream. The radio played and we believed it would hide our thoughts.

And footprints deep marked out new moons of Motherland . . .

Moon . . . ARO5 . . . SOL3 . . . ELD9.

Words. All meaningless words. I wanted to kill myself.

Gramps said, 'Standish, don't think about the past. We'll do what we always did, before the Lushes came.'

What was that, then? Hector brought the light. All he left was the darkness.

Every night we would make out we were off to bed.

'Good night,' Gramps would shout into the room I refused to sleep in. We would sit on the edge of his bed together. Outside a wasp of a car buzzed up and down the road. Midnight, Gramps had worked out, was when the detectives in the wasp car had a break from their duties. Time for a pee, for a bite to eat. That was when Gramps and me would make our way quietly down to Cellar Street.

Fifty-Seven

Before the war – which war, I don't know, there's been so blooming many, all won of course by the great Motherland – anyway before the wars, Gramps had been the senior scene painter at the big opera house in Zone One. Maybe there weren't zones in those days, but that's not the point. No, the point is that once, at the start of the wars, Gramps had painted aeroplanes on the ground. They looked from the sky like the real McCoy. After that war, the Motherland introduced the first programme of re-education. Gramps was forced to attend it for painting those planes. Some of his friends refused to do it. Some were the wrong breed, wrong colour, wrong nationality. They weren't allowed a re-education. The Greenflies needed their maggot meat. As for Gramps, he passed the test. Just.

They – him, Gran and Dad and Mum – were moved here just before I was born. Anyway, that's another way by the by.

Fifty-Eight

The reason I thought about Gramps being a scene painter was because of the wall he had built and painted at the bottom of Cellar Street. You see, Gramps had painted a perfect illusion of a perfect wall. It slid in tight, right next to the alien growth, a giant mushroom-like thing that shone with an unnatural light. It stank as bad as the lines of the Anthem of the Motherland.

Hidden in its pungent, fleshy folds was a small lock and if it was jiggled in a certain way the wall would slide open. Only when the wall was shut again did the lights flicker on in the secret chamber. They ran off an old battery that Mr Lush had rigged up.

It was because of the painted wall that, after the Lushes were taken, Gramps took to working outside in the front garden. He looked as if he was pruning the white roses. Secretly, he was putting in a warning system to tell us if anyone was in the house while we were down in the storeroom in Cellar Street.

I tell you this for a bagful of humbugs, it was eerily deserted under those houses. All we could hear down there was the conversation of rats. A very stubborn thing is your common brown rat. I often wondered how it was the rats became fat when we were so very lean.

Fifty-Nine

A week ago, I came home from school, lost in a daydream. This one involved our flying saucer landing on Planet Juniper. To me it was like having a cinema in my head. I could see Hector touching down, the Juniparians waiting to greet him, smiles on their faces. They were dressed . . . I stopped as I reached the kitchen. Gramps wasn't there. Where the frick-fracking hell was he? Panic flooded through me. I couldn't see straight, couldn't think straight, my head was about to blow a fuse. I rushed outside into the drizzle. He had to be in the vegetable plot, he bloody well had to be in the vegetable plot.

That's when I saw the door to the air raid shelter had been opened.

No! No, no – he hadn't gone through the tunnel? He

wouldn't do that, would he? I couldn't breathe. I couldn't think. All of me felt about to break apart. That was when I spied the enormous boots sticking out of the potting shed.

Sixty

I ran back indoors. Gramps was in the kitchen, taking off his old army coat. I couldn't speak, so I dragged him to the potting shed. Inside, there was this fricking moon man desperately pulling at his huge, steamed-up helmet with his space gloves, his whole body jerking.

Gramps said, 'Go and work in the vegetable patch.'

'But what about –'

'I'll take care of this.'

Frick-fracking hell. I started to dig, did my best to make it look as if I was digging for my supper rather than for our lives. I knew what Gramps was trying to do in the potting shed. Take off the moon man's helmet and fast, otherwise I had better start to dig a grave. I heard a crack and someone gasping for air.

After a bit, Gramps came out of the potting shed and closed the door. Together we went into the kitchen and turned the radio on, razor loud.

And once those feet did tread upon silver sand
And footprints deep marked out new moons of
    Motherland

Gramps whispered over the din, 'We will have to wait until it's dark.'

We waited and waited until night pricked the old sun's balloon.

Only then were we able to bring the moon man into the kitchen.

He seemed giant-tall, very clumsy in all the clothes he wore. It was strange to see close up a face that was so familiar from the posters. Here he was, ELD9, all the hope of the moon landings rinsed from his features. Left in its place were worry lines etched deep into his forehead. The twinkle in his eye extinguished, the cheeky smile a grimace. We sat him down on a chair and gave him tea which he drunk from the corner of his mouth as if each sip was painful.

The moon man said nothing. Then he opened his mouth to show us he had no tongue to speak with.

I guessed that's what they had done to my mum.

Sixty-One

The day Mr Gunnell killed Little Eric Owen and a rocket was launched into space was the day I knew for certain that Gramps and me were unlikely ever to make it out of Zone Seven. Alive, that is. Owning a television is enough of an offence in itself for both of us to be sent away to be re-educated.

By the time we reached our house the front door had been kicked in. There was no need – we never locked it. There was not much point. Inside they had done a very thorough job. There was nothing that hadn't been touched or turned over. It wasn't the broken I minded, I just didn't like who did the breaking. I looked at Gramps. He put his arm around me.

We tried to salvage what we could in the vegetable

patch then worked inside, tidying up the house by candlelight.

Gramps had never taken down the blackout curtains so at least no one could see in, but we knew the detectives had returned. We made a cup of tea and went upstairs to bed. We snuffed out the candle, we waited a hard, hungry hour. I was half-dreaming of spam fritters. Our tummies rumbled. It was after midnight when we finally went down to the cellar, taking some bread and the spam fritters with us.

Gramps put the traps with that day's catch of rats near the stairs that led up to our house. Then we set off again into what you would think was the farthest part of Cellar Street. The pungent smell hit you down there. That was the reason the leather-coat men's dogs were unable to sniff out the moon man. That alien fungus smothered everything with its earthy stench. It even glowed in the dark, looking almost alive, hungry, feeding off the damp and the dark of the house, brittling its bones to the core.

We opened the sliding door. Cripes, I can tell you it was a relief to see the moon man. Not to mention the two hens and the radio Mr Lush had wired up so we could hear, once in a while, the evil empires of the world speak words of comfort to us.

The moon man stood up, hugged Gramps. I went to find the eggs, feed the hens and make sure no rats had got in. Then I lit the Bunsen burner and put the kettle over it. We drunk our tea and ate the bread and the spam fritters. A feast.

The moon man tried to talk to us with drawings. They weren't clever like Gramps' pictures but they told us the story. I could see clearly what was happening behind the wall.

Gramps got up, wiped his mouth on the back of his hand and retuned the radio. It crackled and hissed. He fiddled with the set until we heard The Voice, the only one Gramps trusted to tell the truth. That is, he said, if there is any such thing as a truth. Hard to tell when so much is a lie.

Sixty-Two

The Voice spoke.

'The monstrous Motherland may claim to have launched a rocket to the moon, but our scientists believe that such an expedition is not and will not be possible for many years to come.

'The radiation from the moon's atmosphere will prevent man from landing there. We must not be forced into surrender by propaganda. We must carry on with the fight, regardless. I call on all Obstructors to support the advancing Allies. Sleep easy in your beds. Do not be frightened into believing that the Motherland has the capacity to fire weapons from the moon's surface. Instead concentrate your energies for the final battle. Afterwards we will live in a free world.'

The alarm bell rang, a red-painted light bulb flashed. Gramps looked up and so did I. We both knew what that meant. There was an intruder in the house. We had less than a minute to cover our tracks.

Terror is an odd thing. It has made me panic, it has made me spew, but this time, I felt a calm fury.

Gramps opened the painted wall and the moon man locked it behind us. A torch beam shined into the dark of Cellar Street.

Quickly we picked up the traps. Gramps took two, I took one.

'What are you doing down there?' a man called out.

'Rats,' shouted Gramps.

I was closest to the stairs that led up to the kitchen. The torch shined in my face. The light blinded me and I put up my hand to cover my eyes and by doing that I accidentally pressed the release button on the trap and the rat leaped up the stairs, past the intruder into the kitchen. A shot rang out.

Gramps was by my side. He went up the stairs first, carrying the cages with the other two rats in them. In the kitchen, sitting at the broken table, was a man we had never seen before. He laid down his revolver and lit a cigarette. The rat was dead in the corner.

'Mr Treadwell,' said the man. 'I have come to take the visitor to safety. We haven't much time.'

Gramps and I both knew that if this man really did belong to the Obstructors, he would never have shot the rat. The gun had no silencer on it. The noise would have been heard outside, loud and with bells on. The detectives in their car would have to be deaf, daft or both not to have heard and come running.

The man was a joker.

Sixty-Three

You see, that intruder was too well-dressed. Much like the dead rats he was too clean, too well-fed.

'I don't know who you are,' said Gramps, 'but I don't think you should be here. I would like you to leave. Standish, go and tell the detectives outside we have an Obstructor here.'

The man picked up his revolver. 'I am here to help you.'

'I don't believe it,' said Gramps.

'I think,' I said, 'you are one of the people who broke into our house today and found nothing.'

That got the man agitated. He took out another cigarette. You don't see many of those. Tobacco was for the few. No freedom fighter would ever smoke those smokes. They have the crest of the Motherland printed on them. The man was a prick if he thought we were that thick.

Sixty-Four

It was pitch-black outside. Only that eyesore of a building at the end of our road was lit up, starbright, earth-bound. I crept towards the waiting car in which the two detectives sat. I made them jump out of their seats. One wound down his steamed-up window, his mouth full of sausage. The car smelled of farts.

'We have an intruder in the house,' I said. 'You'd better come.'

The supposed Obstructor made a feeble attempt to run.

We watched as the car did a three-point turn and gave chase. It was pathetic. Even we could see they all knew one another. The 'Obstructor' shrugged his shoulders. The back door of the wasps' car was opened for him.

I tell you this, if he had been the genuine McCoy, they would have shot him to where no kingdom comes.

In the kitchen Gramps had his coat on.

'What are you doing?' I said.

He shook his head and puts his fingers to his lips.

'Taking the rat out.'

But I knew he wasn't. He was off. Where, I didn't know, couldn't say. I wanted to cling on to that coat of his, beg him to stay. He wouldn't. I could see by the look in his eyes that he was going to go, come what may.

Sixty-Five

I slept on and off with my head on my arms at the kitchen table. I hadn't dared move. Call it superstition. It must have been about six that morning when I woke. It was light, had been light for a long time. Still Gramps hadn't returned. To tell the fricking truth, I was no longer calm. I was bloody terrified.

The moon man emerged from the cellar, relieved to see me. He still wore his gravity boots, which he didn't need as there was plenty of gravity there. Too much. In fact, I thought a little less of it might be a good idea.

I made tea for the moon man while he rinsed his mouth in salty water. It was all the medicine we had to offer. That and the rest of the aspirins. I saw him wince. I knew he shouldn't be up here, it was far too dangerous.

But I didn't want him to leave, didn't want to be on my own, waiting. He sat down. I still found it hard to look at the word sewn on his space suit: ELD9.

He wrote the word 'Gramps' and I said, 'He's not here.'

I could see that worried him. I tell you this, it worried me too. I wasn't even going to think of the 'what if' scenarios.

Sixty-Six

We sat in silence, the moon man and me. I knew he couldn't speak but there is silence and there is silence, if you get my meaning. I'll tell you this for nothing: I was born into a frick-fracking nightmare. The only way out was in my head. In my head there are Croca-Colas, Cadillacs. There is Planet Juniper and Hector to rescue us all.

My bones nearly jumped free from my muscles when I heard a noise in the back garden. The moon man disappeared back to Cellar Street. I washed up the cups, put them away.

I don't think I was breathing when Gramps said, 'Let me in.'

'Where have you been?' I asked as I opened the back door. His face was all smoky, his shirt torn and burnt.

He wasn't wearing his hat or his coat. No. Miss Phillips was. She stood behind him. She looked as if she had been beaten up pretty badly.

'What happened?'

Gramps just put the kettle on and made tea. Miss Phillips was shaking.

'They set fire to her house. I knew they would,' he said. 'It was only a matter of time.'

I took a bowl of water to the table. That was one fricking bruise she had.

Gramps lifted up Miss Phillips' face towards his and gently wiped away the smoke. I watched all this and felt that there was something more there.

When she winced, he said softly, 'It's all right, love.'

I thought I understood. Well, I thought I did, but hell's bells, I wasn't that sure.

I placed the cup of tea near her.

She put both her hands round the cup and stared at the grain of the table. Gramps was now at the sink, washing his face and hands. I turned on the radio again. It was playing music for the workers of the Motherland.

Quietly, she said, 'Thank you.'

Sixty-Seven

Gramps returned to where Miss Phillips was sitting. He took off her hat. Miss Phillips' hair had always been long, neatly wound into a bun. It was now so short it stood up in tufts, and blood was mixed up in it.

I knew that haircut and I knew exactly what that haircut meant. It was what they did to the Obstructors. Strip them naked, take away all their clothes, cut their hair off. If it was a woman they didn't bother to kill her, not outright. They left that to the young, hungry vultures. The Hans Fielders and the boys from the torture lounge.

It was a slower death but it gave them a bit of practice in killing. You couldn't be squeamish if you joined the Youth of the Motherland. The Mothers for Purity would be ashamed of them if they hadn't mastered the art of butchery before they'd left school. I mean, it's one of those rights of way you have to go through. It certainly showed up the fags from the thugs. A thug would have beaten Miss Phillips' brains out for breakfast. Goodness knows what he would have done to her by lunchtime.

It was only then that it dawned on me that Miss Phillips had protected me at school. Like the time Mr Gunnell tried to make the whole class join the Youth of the Motherland. It was Miss Phillips who had argued that they wouldn't want a boy like me, a boy who had trouble tying his shoelaces. She probably told Mr Hellman I was making progress in Miss Connolly's class. Why didn't I work that out before?

I emptied the bowl of dirty water and refilled it.

Gramps tilted her face to his and kissed her. Well, I wasn't expecting that. I mean, Gramps is too old for all that. Surely when you are in your fifties that kind of thing stops? That myth had just been torpedoed out of the water. Gramps put his arm round Miss Phillips and she rested her head on his stomach.

'So that's it,' I said. They both looked at me as if they had forgotten I was there. 'You and Miss Phillips. I mean, how long have you been . . . courting?'

They both smiled.

'Three years.'

Well, you could have knocked me sideways with a feather. Three years.

'It's been hard since the Lushes disappeared,' said Gramps.

I suppose me sleeping on top of his bed like a dog hadn't helped.

Miss Phillips said, 'Harry told me about the moon man and we have been doing our best to make contact with the Obstructors so that the information can be moved up the line. But Zone Seven is closed off from the outside world.'

The music stopped and the Voice of the Motherland broke in.

'Today, the leaders of the evil empires agreed to convene in our great capital Tyker to see our achievements with their own eyes. Earth will behold the first pictures ever to be taken of our new-won territory, the moon.

'Praise be the Motherland.'

Sixty-Eight

There was an unmistakable cacophony outside our house. Boots hitting the pavement, car doors slamming, people shouting. Just one sound was missing from the orchestra of fear. They hadn't brought the dogs with them, not this time. I was glued to the floor. We had been caught. It was all over.

Only when Gramps said fiercely, 'Standish, move!' did I unfreeze.

We hid Miss Phillips upstairs at the back of Mum and Dad's old monster of a wardrobe.

'That'll be the first place they'll look,' I said.

Gramps just pulled open the wardrobe door.

'No, the Greenflies aren't that smart. They are getting greener by the day.'

Gramps was going into his bedroom when I remembered his coat. I ran back, took it from Miss Phillips and raced down the stairs. Another car screeched to a halt.

I hung up the coat, checked the table then opened the front door before they could kick it in again.

I wasn't expecting the leather-coat man. He was yesterday's problem. What surprised me most about seeing him was this: up to that moment my legs had been river reeds which threatened to collapse under me. But the sight of this git put the bull between my teeth good and proper.

'It's becoming routine,' said the leather-coat man. 'Every day I'm faced with Standish Treadwell. Where is your grandfather?'

'Asleep,' I said. 'Why do you want him?'

He slapped me across the face with his leather glove.

'I ask the questions.'

He was speaking to me again as if I was stupid and to oblige I said, really slowly, 'Yes, sir.'

I could see the Greenflies waiting behind him for the order to come charging in.

'Mr Treadwell,' said the leather-coat man.

I turned to see Gramps stiffening that gammy leg of his. He pottered down the stairs real slow in his old pyjamas and his patchwork dressing-gown, yawning.

'Why are you here?' he asked. 'You broke everything yesterday.'

It was not hard to see that the leather-coat man was a kettle of liquid fury about to reach boiling point. He sat on one of the broken chairs. It rocked back and forth. I hoped the bloody thing would break under him. He took to slapping the table, slapping it with his leather gloves.

Gramps just let out a sigh soiled with weariness. 'I'm an old man. I try to survive with my grandson, nothing more. Why do you keep hounding us? We have done nothing wrong.'

The leather-coat man didn't answer. He waved in the Greenflies. Gramps was right about one thing, they were very young. Just a bit older than me. Upstairs, downstairs, they went, into the cellar. An infestation of them.

I thought, well, this is it, it's all over apart from the wailing and gnashing of teeth. Louder than the rats in the woodwork were those soldiers. The walls seemed papier mâché thin. The floorboards shook.

The leather-coat man sat there, smack-smack-smacking his gloves on the table. He stopped only to take out a cigarette and light it.

Finally, he said, 'I want you to tell me where he is.'

'Who?' asked Gramps.

The leather-coat man was stuck on the fly-paper of an unanswerable question.

The gloves hit the table again. The long silence was broken. The leather-coat man said, 'We took a television away from this house.'

'Yes,' said Gramps. 'It was from the time we were allowed to have them.'

Much to my amazement the leather-coat man didn't answer.

I realised that Gramps must have pulled that TV apart so that no one would suspect that we had seen the land of Croca-Colas, where all the colour lived, where people were having a ball.

The leather-coat man stubbed out his cigarette on the table, leaving a round, burnt hole. Maybe it was that burnt hole on the table that gave me the idea. You see, I saw in its pattern a stone. That's when the idea floated into my brain.

The Greenflies came up from the cellar. They looked as if they'd done their job to the letter, their uniforms more grey than green. I knew they hadn't found the moon man because if they had we would have heard their triumphant shouts. Instead they brought up the rat traps.

The man in charge of the Greenflies came down the stairs. He didn't look too happy to whisper what he had to whisper to the leather-coat man.

'Nothing? Nothing? Are you sure?' shouted the leather-coat man.

'Nothing, sir.'

The odd thing about being that close to the edge was that I could see that both Gramps and I were resigned to the fall. It was almost as if it was fate's game, not ours. She was the one dealing the cards. I think I knew then what was going on behind the wall in the garden. They had built the moon in that hideous building, the one once called the people's palace.

That was when my idea became a plan. I thought about it from all angles. I almost left the room – it was really taking shape.

'You are both under house arrest.' The leather-coat

man interrupted my thoughts, which was irritating as I had spun the whole thing in my head, 360 degrees.

'Are you listening, Standish Treadwell?' he said.

I have this effect on people. They think I'm not paying attention when I am.

To the train-track mind of the leather-coat man, I appeared to be Vacant. Vacant was the word Mr Gunnell liked to use about me. Vacant I might look, but I am not. Hector and I spent ages working on this look of mine. You don't get to sit right at the back of the class if you're stand-out smart.

'You and your grandfather will be removed at 06.30 hours tomorrow. You are being offered salvation over annihilation. You will both be sent on a re-education course.'

No, we bloody well won't. He was lying. We were going to be wiped out, maggot meat.

'Each of you can pack one suitcase,' he continued. 'Under no circumstances are you to leave these premises.'

The jerk. This was our house, our home.

The Greenflies waited until the leather-coat man strode out to his black, bluebottle car.

We stood on the step, Gramps and me, as if we were

saying goodbye to friends who had popped in for tea. We watched the last of the Greenflies climb back into the trucks. They drove off, leaving only the car with the detectives watching us from behind their dark glasses.

If I were a Juniparian, which I'm not, I would save the world. Still, I did have a plan. It was based on a story I once heard about this giant and a boy about my age, my height, and a stone. Just one small stone shot from a catapult hit that giant between the eyes. He dropped down dead, the giant did. I tell you, it was such a foolish idea I thought it might be foolproof.

Miss Phillips came down the stairs. She wore a pair of Gramps' trousers and one of his shirts.

She looked at him and smiled. 'One of the Greenflies said if anyone was hiding in there they would have closed the door.'

I thought the difficult part of my plan would be to convince Gramps and Miss Phillips that it would work. That all I needed to defeat the Motherland was one stone.

And the stone-thrower would be me.

Sixty-Nine

There was much I learned that day about Gramps. For a start, as well as having Miss Phillips, he had a transmitter. I still can't make my way round it. How I could be so naive about both? Apparently the transmitter broke over a year back. You can't take a thing like that to the shop to get it mended. It was Mr Lush who fixed it and made sure that even if the Motherland picked up the signal, the code would automatically be scrambled.

A day ago I didn't know there was a transmitter behind a wooden panel in the kitchen wall. A day ago, I thought of Gramps as old. Today he is a silver fox with a cunning tail.

Seventy

Miss Phillips sat in the secret chamber in Cellar Street. Cripes, she is clever. She could read the moon man's notes even though they were in the language of the East. Gramps hadn't been able to make tail or head of them. He sat on a stool next to her with the earphones on, patiently trying to get a message through to the Obstructors. All was dead.

By lunchtime there had been nothing.

In the end Gramps stopped trying. We ate scrambled eggs with stale toast. Miss Phillips hardly touched her food. She had lost her appetite. I think it was to do with the moon man's notes. He wasn't eating either.

'What do they say?' asked Gramps, squeezing Miss Phillips' hand.

'Let me just go over them once more,' she said.

I knew she was stalling.

'They have had built a huge film set of the moon in the old palace, haven't they?' I said.

'Yes,' said Miss Phillips. 'They will film the rocket landing on the moon there, and the first moon walk. Afterwards, everyone who has worked on the project will be disposed of. That includes the scientists, the workers, and the astronauts. They have already dug the mass graves.'

I interrupted her. 'How did the moon man find our tunnel?' The moon man wrote and Miss Phillips translated. I could see she was not sure if she should tell me the answer. I knew it already. Still I said, 'Go on – tell me.'

Miss Phillips hesitated.

I said, 'He saw Hector, didn't he?'

Seventy-One

The moon man nodded then started to write again on the notepad. Miss Phillips looked more and more uncomfortable.

'Read it out, love,' said Gramps.

She had a good voice. Nothing of what she read would be good in any voice.

'In the beginning I believed I was involved in a genuine space mission. Then one of the scientists who had built the first prototype rocket confided in me that the belt of radiation around the moon would fry us alive. The scientist disappeared soon after. For no reason I could work out, I was sent here to Zone Seven and I realised that the scientist was right. This was the greatest hoax in the history of mankind. I asked too many questions and that's when they silenced me. But they still needed my face. I had to escape. I took a stroll near the bottom of the wall where the bushes are wild. That was where I spotted a red football. And at the same time a boy emerged from the earth, or so it seemed. I knew the boy. The boy knew me.'

'How?' I interrupted again.

Miss Phillips translated. 'I recognised him as the son of the scientist responsible for building the first prototype, the scientist who told me it was impossible to send a man to the moon.'

'Mr Lush?' said Gramps.

The moon man nodded.

'Are they in there?' asked Gramps. 'Are they all right?'

He made his hand into the shape of a gun. I don't think any of us wanted to hear the answer that the moon man wrote down.

Miss Phillips' voice was almost a whisper as she read out his words. 'Mrs Lush was shot the minute they arrived, in front of Mr Lush and their son. We all witnessed it.'

'Why?' I shouted. 'Why?' The question hung unanswered.

It was a slow business, what with Miss Phillips having to put all the moon man's writing into words we could understand.

'Punishment for not cooperating.'

'What about Hector?'

I waited forever until Miss Phillips said, 'They chopped off his little finger after they killed Mrs Lush, and told Mr Lush if he refused to do all that was asked of him another finger would go, and another.'

'Is Hector alive?'

The moon man nodded. He held up nine fingers.

'So he lost the one?'

The moon man nodded again.

Gramps almost didn't hear the beeps coming through on the transmitter. At long last, someone, somewhere was receiving us. The beeps sounded like the heartbeat of a civilisation we had feared might well be dead.

We had orders from the Obstructers to be ready to leave at eleven o'clock that evening. We were to make our way to the farthest end of Cellar Street, in the direction of the double-breasted houses.

That was when I said, 'I'm not coming.'

Seventy-Two

'You have to, Standish,' said Gramps. 'You can't stay here.'

'I'm going to rescue Hector,' I said. 'Throw my stone into the face of the Motherland. Show the world the moon landing is a hoax.'

'Standish,' said Gramps, 'your head is full of dreams.'

So I told them my plan. I told them if I could get near the moon set then when the astronaut took his first steps I would try to break free from the other workers and stand on the moon surface in front of the cameras. I would hold up a piece of paper with the word HOAX written on it. Then the free world would know it was all a lie.

'What? And be shot dead?' said Gramps, his face full of storm clouds of rage.

To tell the truth, I hadn't thought about what would happen after I held up my sign. I'd work it out then and there. That bit didn't strike me as something you could plan. There were, as always, too many what ifs.

'If a giant can be brought down by a stone, can't I do the same?'

'No,' said Gramps. 'No. It's a bloody stupid idea.'

Surprisingly, Miss Phillips said, 'Maybe, Harry, he can get in there, do something . . .'

'And bloody well be killed into the bargain,' said Gramps. He was spitting angry. It was not all to do with my plan, of that I was sure. It had a lot to do with the Lushes and Hector. He said, 'I have lost my family, my friends. I am not about to sacrifice my grandson.'

Miss Phillips put her hand on Gramps' arm.

'Our chances of escaping are tiny,' she said. 'If we are all killed then what would we have achieved? No one would ever know it was a hoax. The leaders of the free world will swallow this lie and by doing so they will make the Motherland all-powerful.'

I could see Gramps was doing his best not to listen.

'Harry,' Miss Phillips said softly, 'whatever happens you will never be alone, I promise.'

I felt relieved about that. I wanted to say more.

All I managed was, 'Miss Phillips is right. You will never be without me either, whether I go with you or not.'

Gramps was shaking as if an earthquake was erupting from his tummy button. Tears, the tears he said he would never cry, rolled down his face in a cascade of rage. I hugged him. I held him tight. I had the strength to do that.

He clung to me. I would remember that until the end, whatever, whenever the end might be.

He let me go, turned away, his shoulders shaking, a sob rising out of him.

Still I felt certain I could be the stone-thrower.

The moon man went to Gramps and put his hand on his shoulder, to give him gravity when everything was floating away. Then he scribbled something on the notepad and handed it to Miss Phillips.

She read it out loud, slowly.

It said what Gramps didn't want to hear. Neither did Miss Phillips. For all her courage I could see that.

'Standish is our only hope.'

Seventy-Three

I spent the rest of the afternoon with the moon man and Miss Phillips. Gramps went back upstairs. He didn't want to hear any more. I don't blame him. I had to, if I was ever to throw my stone.

What the moon man told me was no longer written on a notepad but scribbled into my brain. I knew exactly what was going on behind that wall. I had the map. I had the knowledge.

Seventy-Four

I return upstairs to wait with Gramps until it's time for me to leave. Miss Phillips and the moon man stay put in Cellar Street.

Gramps has been making full-size cut-out figures. Why, I haven't a clue. He is sitting on the floor staring at nothing, surrounded by bits of cardboard. I think it is all too much for him. Tell you this, it's all too much for me.

I sit next to him. There are no words. His thoughts are too loud for me. I block them out by telling myself the story of what has happened up to this moment. The moment Gramps and I are sitting together on this curled-up lino. I take a photo of him with my mind's eye, one I can carry with me. I am trying to see what he looked like when he was younger, before the crust of age and anxiety grew over him. His hands are big, they look like the roots of trees, well-worn, well-used. They can paint walls to fool Greenflies, make whole all that is broken. They are hands that I'm walking away from. I know what Gramps is thinking. He is wondering if he will have the strength to let me go. I'm wondering if I will have the strength to leave him.

What would happen if we sat here dead still, did nothing? Would time leave us alone, pass us by?

Bring down the curtain.

Bring up the credits.

The end.

Seventy-Five

Frick-fracking hell! That rat-a-tat-tat quick-started time, made its heart, our hearts, do a round of the racecourse. We both raise our heads. I spring to my feet. The detectives usually aren't that polite. Knocking is something they don't do much of. No, this is a different kettle of shit altogether. They're checking up on us, want the blackout curtains down. They remind us we have to be ready to leave at six-thirty the next morning.

'Yes,' I say, hoping they haven't spied Gramps sitting on the lino, his face a blank, two cardboard cut-outs on the floor beside him.

I close the front door as Gramps gets slowly to his feet.

'Time,' he says. 'It's time, Standish.'

He attaches the two cut-out figures to two broken chairs. Now I see what he was up to. The silhouettes look very much like me and Gramps. He is bloody clever at things like this, always one step ahead. He knew those detectives would want to see in. It's twilight and the flickering candles do their trick, make those cardboard cut-outs look almost realistic. At least they will fool the detectives, make them think we are quietly awaiting our fate.

Just before ten o'clock we crawl across the kitchen floor towards the stairs. It occurs to me that in five hours the only words Gramps has spoken are, 'It's time, Standish, it's time.'

Seventy-Six

In the bedroom that once belonged to my parents Gramps hands me a wide belt he has made. It is to go under my clothes. On both sides in Gramps' beautiful hand is written large and bold the word HOAX. Do you know, I think this is what he has been doing while I was in the cellar. The cardboard figures were an afterthought.

'I haven't a catapult to give you. This will have to do,' he says.

I don't say what I want to say. Perhaps it's better.

I get dressed in the rags Gramps has found for me. Rags that would embarrass a scarecrow. Gramps brings out Mum's old make-up bag. He gently puts chalky paste on my face, darkens the sockets round my eyes, rubs mud into my hands.

When I look in that monster wardrobe mirror I see a ghost. My ghost.

Seventy-Seven

Miss Phillips has come up from Cellar Street and is sitting in the shadows on the top stair.

I know why she is there. To say the unsayable goodbye.

Gramps opens the back door and turns towards her.

Miss Phillips' hard no-nonsense face is bruised, tender-wet with tears. She nods.

Outside, the moon is up over the wall. Gramps pulled down the air raid shelter after the moon man appeared. All that is left of it is neatly stacked to hide the tunnel entrance. He removes the sheets of corrugated iron, ready for me to get through before he puts them all back. So that it will look like nothing has happened.

Here it is, a grave in the earth, ready and waiting for me. There's no turning back, not now. I am in no-man's-land.

No land anybody would fricking want to be in, that's for sure.

I kiss Gramps.

I don't expect him to say a word.

He says, 'Standish, I'm proud of you.'

Seventy-Eight

I know I'm dead. The only question is how I die.

I am seeing what Hector saw when he broke through. The hatch is completely hidden among all the brambles and stinging nettles. I managed to rip my shorts and scratch my legs when I scrabbled out from under all that tangle of nature.

I dust as much of the dirt off me as I can, the rest I rub into my skin. I look pretty filthy and there is blood dripping down my legs. I climb up to where the meadow was. Now it's a battlefield of lorry tracks and wounded earth. In the distance is that ugly old palace, its huge glass window still staring.

I know which way to go. I have the moon man's map engraved in my mind, though the latrines are farther away than I imagined. The light is so bright you might convince yourself it was the middle of the day rather than the oncoming night.

It's funny how in one's head everything seems so simple. I had it all worked out. I would break in, find Hector, throw my stone and together we would escape. It's the fricking reality that destroys plans. I make my way toward the latrines, which aren't far from that atrocity of a building. I could find them blindfolded – the smell is shit awful. I see the searchlight, an eye in the sky to winkle me out. Here goes, Standish, here goes.

'Stop!' one of the guards shouts as its beam pins me to the spot.

There is the sound of running feet. Two Greenflies grab me and drag me before a man whose face I can't see – the light behind him is too bright.

Please, I am thinking, don't let this be all over before it's begun. Don't let this be the leather-coat man. I cover my eyes.

'Turn the light away,' the man shouts.

He is outlined in electric yellow. I am relieved to see an officer who isn't the leather-coat man.

He is yelling, 'What the fuck are you doing here?'

And I say, in my best Motherland tongue, 'Taking a shit, sir.'

'Why down there?'

'Have you seen the latrines? Even the rats are killed off by the smell.'

I am expecting a slap for my cheek.

Instead he says, 'A good shit? It must have been by the look of your legs.' He laughs. 'So you don't like the facilities?'

I think it's best not to answer that one. He doesn't look that stable, this hand-grenade of an officer.

'Are you on the day shift?'

I nod.

The officer marches me towards a hut, where an enormous woman is sitting in a chair. Behind her, a sacking curtain masks what lies inside. She stands up. So does the chair, stuck out at an angle from her bottom.

She is wearing a matron's uniform but I don't think she has much to do with nursing.

The officer is happily yelling at the fat woman. It's not worth translating – anyone can get the general gist of what he is saying – but it gives me time to see more clearly what is beyond the open doors of the palace. It looks to me like the moon has collided with Zone Seven.

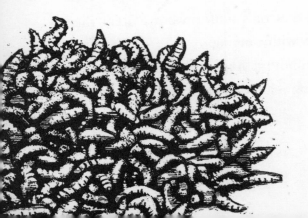

Seventy-Nine

The moon man told me there were thousands of starving people working here. I can see a lot of figures standing on the dark side of the moon. I am now looking properly at a film set which is the most important film set ever to be built, one that will shape all our lives, change history. The world is about to swallow one huge, inedible lie. And I, Standish Treadwell, am the only one with a plan.

The fat woman returns to her post, cursing the officer under her breath as he walks away. I notice she has a whip which has fallen to the floor and I feel a great temptation to kick it away from her. But I don't.

'Number?' she shouts at me.

'Um . . . not good with remembering numbers,' I say. Stupid will work well for me here.

She pulls back the curtain. And I'm thinking, roll up, roll up, welcome to Hell's waiting room.

Bunks upon bunks, nothing more than two boards to each bed, no covers, nothing. They are all sleeping in their clothes, even in their shoes. They look like shrunken corpses, the clothes the only solid reminder that they once filled them out with purpose.

There isn't a spare bed.

I'm thinking about crawling under one of the bunks when a women says, 'Here, love, you'd better share with me.'

She is painfully thin, her eyes hollow.

'Where are you from?' she asks.

'I'm lost,' I say.

'Aren't we all.'

Such a cruel nation is the monstrous Motherland. I'm amazed no one has risen up to throttle the bitch.

Eighty

I don't remember much until the lights come on. A bell rings and one by one each of the bunk beds is emptied. Everyone stands robot-still. The Greenflies have furious-looking Alsatians pulling at their leashes. We line up to wash at a pump.

The woman who let me stay on the bare boards with her says, 'Drink the water. Wipe your face but drink as much water as you can.'

That's not as simple as it sounds. The guards don't want any water-drinking going on. We line up again. Each of us is given one slice of bread balanced on a mug of black tea. We are marched into the palace as the figures I saw last night march pass us in the opposite direction, too tired to lift their feet. They are going to sleep on the hard wooden bunks we've just left.

Frick-fracking hell. Once you're inside that atrocity of a building and you see that moon for yourself, that's when you realise it fills the whole of this huge, ugly beast. There are men in white coats walking about taking exact measurements of everything.

Our orders for today are to get the sky backcloths in place and position the stars where they should be. Details are things the Motherland likes a lot. Paperwork and details. Everyone lines up. I tell you this, it looks so unreal. A city of moon workers. At least I won't be noticed in this huge crowd. According to the moon man the only way to get near the set is to volunteer, which no ever one does. The reason being that if you fail or one of the officers takes against you, that adds up to a bullet in the head. And you can't argue with a bullet that final.

I might have to think that one through again. The one about volunteering, on account of my courage doesn't seem to have woken up with me. I hope Gramps, Miss Phillips and the moon man got away for I don't think I will.

'You there,' comes a voice.

'Me?'

'Yes, you.'

I am pulled out of the crowd. I stand on the edge of the moon, feeling its silvery dust through the hole in my shoe.

'Did you hear what I said?'

This officer has a revolver in his hand and it looks like it might need a bit of shooting practice. I can see why Mr Gunnell was so keen to join this load of maggot makers.

'Yes,' I say.

Because although I was definitely thinking about other things I also was listening. They are wanting volunteers. The only bit I missed – which was a pity – was what they wanted volunteers for.

I put my hand up. The officer with a gun and the need for a head to fire it into looks almost disappointed. One of the Greenflies pulls me away.

Eighty-One

There are two other boys of about my age who didn't volunteer. Still they are dragged out of the crowd. I hear a woman yell out a boy's name. The boy, older than me, flinches as he hears her. We are marched away from the moon set. Frick-fracking hell, I should have paid a bit more attention. Maybe I volunteered to clean out those stinking latrines. We are now in bright sunlight, and looking into a car park full of the silver lozenges of lorries that the moon man told me and Miss Phillips about. Yes, see, once all these thousands of moon workers have done their jobs they will be given a nice bar of soap and a nice gas bath.

The more I see of all this, the less optimistic I feel that I, Standish Treadwell, can do anything other than become like everyone else here. Maggot meat. The two other boys with me are so thin that they make me stand out. This worries me. Still they are not yet as skeletal as others I've seen. Somehow this doesn't comfort me. What if it's a trick? What if the leather-coat man found the tunnel last night, has arrested Gramps, Miss Phillips and the moon man, knows what I'm doing here? The place is swarming with Greenflies and officers. Never have I seen as many as I have today. I think I have entered an insect nest.

We march past the latrines, past the waiting lorries. That's a relief. At least, I hope it's a relief.

Hunger makes you see things leanly. This is no way to live and those silver lozenges are no way to die.

Eighty-Two

The laboratory is a thing of efficient ugliness with a huge flag of the Motherland flying above it. I know this is where they do their experiments. The moon man told me.

The three of us are marched up the stairs and down a long corridor. We are weighed and measured. No surprise – I weigh the most. I just hope it doesn't give me away. Each of us has a number pinned to him and we are ushered into a thin, long room with what must be a two-way mirror at one end. We are told to face one way, then sideways. The faceless one watching from behind the glass calls out the numbers until I am the only one left.

Either this means I have won a prize, or Number Five

your time is up. I am trying to look on the sunny side of this sinking boat. But I am shit scared.

A guard walks me down more corridors. Two swing doors with portholes open into a large, high room. Up near the ceiling is a metal beam with a rope dangling from it. There are sandbags on the floor. In the wall opposite is a window – I am being watched without being able to see who is doing the watching. For a moment I think, hell, I am about to be hanged and I have never drunk Croca-Cola, never driven a Cadillac, and never, ever kissed a girl. All these nevers are what I'm going to take away with me.

I am clipped into a harness which is fastened by another clip to the end of the rope. Then the sandbags are attached to the harness so I am weighted down. A man in an astronaut suit and gravity boots like our moon man wears, but a lot cleaner, enters the room. His face is lost behind the shimmer of a golden glass visor. He, too, is being attached to something. What, I can't see.

A man in a white coat tells me, 'You must pull up and down on the rope when we say so.'

I do and I see why they wanted me. My feet leave the ground. The astronaut at the other end is suspended from the rope by nearly invisible wires. I'm not sure how, but by pushing my weight up and down the man rises from the floor just enough to make it look like there's no gravity. The rope glides this way and that along the beam.

After a bit I feel too thirsty to go on. It's hot in this harness, I can tell you. I stop. I am not jumping up and down any more. A guard comes over to me. He might be Mr Gunnell's twin brother. That's if Mr Gunnell had a twin brother, one that doesn't wear a toupee. They both have the same 'I will kill you' look about them. They both have flat backs of heads.

'Move.' He pokes at me. Meat hung up to be screwered.

The astronaut stands waiting. I don't care. I want a glass of water.

Eighty-Three

What am I doing, I ask myself. For the guard looks ready to make mincemeat of me. I have ruined my only chance of carrying out my plan, my one and only chance of showing Gramps' words to the world. Fool. For what? A glass of water.

This is what I'm thinking as the astronaut leaves the room. A white-coated man appears. He calls the guard over. The guard too leaves the room so here I am, just the white-coated man and me. He stands there staring straight – no, more crooked, I would say – at me as if I was an alien species. I feel like telling him I am from Planet Juniper. I don't. Instead I stare down at the cement floor.

I look up when he says, 'You are the first one who can do this. Unlike the others you are healthy.'

'What does that mean?' I ask.

'You have stamina.'

'I'm one of the new intake, sir.'

He doesn't answer. Maybe I shouldn't have said that.

It was a relief, I can tell you, to see the guard come back with a glass of water and a hunk of brown bread.

Brown bread.

You're dead.

I drink. I eat.

I am doing my best to think the bread and the water are good signs. That they mean I'll be clipped back into the harness. Except I'm not. The guard – the one that looks like Mr Gunnell's brother – takes me away. Away to where? That's what's giving me the heebie-jeebies. My head hurts just thinking about it. Now I'm sure the leather-coat man has found the tunnel, put two and two together, made five. Maybe the white-coated man reported me. At least we are still walking. I think that's a good sign. We are walking back towards the moon set. Only then does it hit me. Frick-fracking hell! Perhaps I was no good at being the weight at the end of gravity and I am being sent to join the thousands of workers who are brushing the moon surface smooth. I comfort myself that it might be better from that angle to rush out with my sign than be stuck in a harness.

Well, that thought just went out the window.

I am shown a trench in a crease of the moon's surface. It's long and thin and curves round a bend. It's deep enough for me to run back and forth without being seen.

Down there is a man in brown overalls. I am dropped into the trench and a harness like that of a rucksack is clipped on me at the front. I watch how he does it. Then he attaches invisible wires to my harness.

I can't see a frick-fracking thing from down here. Then suddenly my feet lift off the ground and the brown overall moves me about as if I'm a puppet.

Which, when you think about it, I am. I am the dead weight that makes the astronaut look weightless. I bob back and forth in the trench until I can bob no more.

Eighty-Four

It must be late. I am now too light-headed to be much use. Finally, I am unclipped. I make mental notes. The clip with the invisible wire – that's not going to be too hard to undo. What is worrying me is how the frick-fracking hell am I going to climb out of this trench fast enough? If I can't do that I will never be able to hold up my sign and the world will never know.

I'm beginning to think this volunteering idea might not have been my brightest. Then to my humongous relief the brown overall man shows me steps that I hadn't seen, fixed to the side of the trench. I note where they are and try to work out how long it will take me to climb up them – after I've managed to free myself from the invisible wire. All I have to do then is make it to the moon surface as fast as I can take my belt off.

Still I have no plans for the 'then what?' Just to get that far would be something to shout home about.

I emerge from the trench to find Mr Gunnell's double-gangster waiting.

Eighty-Five

'You're lucky,' says the guard. 'The last boy died.'

He walks me down a metal spiral staircase which seems to go round and round and on forever. At the bottom there is an endless white corridor, the lights running along the middle in small shades that throw triangles of blinding brightness. On each side are rows of metal doors with thick submarine glass at the top. Still we keep walking. I'm not sure where the lucky comes into this. The guard's steel-capped boots echo the sound of a marching army. Apart from our footsteps there is an eerie silence down here. It seems to be deserted. I feel as if I'm being buried alive. The place smells of metal and earth.

And still we keep walking.

I wonder what the guard meant. Am I dead or is there a tomorrow? I don't ask him. I can see it would give him too much pleasure not to tell me. He stops at a door that looks the same as all the others. Unlocks it then pushes it open. I can see nothing but blackness. Maybe I'm right – I will be left to perish here and no one will give a damn.

The guard shoves me inside and the door shuts behind me with the sound of forever in its locks.

I'm trying my best to see when I can't see a thing. I have no idea how big or small the cell is, just feel its dank darkness. It takes me a while to work out I'm not alone. Someone else is here. The someone else speaks.

'So have they got your parents too?' this someone says. 'How loved are you?' I don't answer. Even broken, I know that voice. 'The last boy wasn't loved that much. You see, they killed him.'

I edge nearer, my hands out before me.

'Stay away from me,' he says. I keep going. 'I said stay away!'

I don't stop until I think I am near him and he'll be able to hear me whisper.

'Hector,' I say, 'it's Standish.'

Eighty-Six

I can't see Hector. I can only hear his voice. He is a huddle, a shadow in the corner. I sit down next to him.

He moves closer.

I know he is hurt.

I know him better than I know my own face.

I know what he is thinking.

He is thinking what the frick-fracking hell is Standish doing here?

'What have they done to you?' I ask.

'Nothing too bad,' he says. 'I still have eight fingers left.'

'You should have ten.'

'My little finger went to my papa after they shot Mama.'

His voice is weak. I can hardly hear him.

'I don't understand,' I say. 'Why?'

'Because they wanted to show Papa they meant business this time. That if he refused to cooperate with the bigwigs again then they would kill me too. But slower.'

He is having trouble breathing.

'What did your papa do?' I ask.

He takes his time. It's a secret not to be spoken of. Though I know the answer. I will only believe it if Hector tells me.

'He was a government scientist,' he whispers. 'Papa dreamed he would send a man to the moon. The President liked that dream. But then Papa refused to work for the President because of the way the Motherland treats its workers.' Hector's voice is faint and he tries to catch his breath. 'They call people like my father a sleeper. We knew that one day Papa would have to be woken. They needed him.'

I suppose getting a fake moon to look like the real thing with a spaceship that could land on it and an astronaut to walk on it might take a scientist or two.

Hector speaks very softly. 'If Papa does what they ask him I'll get fed, my bandage will be changed. If he doesn't then I will lose another finger.'

Eighty-Seven

The lights go on so suddenly that it feels as if someone has punched me. Hector opens his eyes. I think maybe they've been listening. Did I say too much? Did Hector? It's so bright that for a moment I am blinded all over again. Hector pulls away. When he comes into focus he is looking at me as if I am some sort of apparition.

'I hoped you were just a dream,' he says. 'A good dream, come to comfort me.'

I see Hector clearly now. He looks transparent. His bandages are grubby, new blood seeps through. He's going to be all right, though. I know he is going to be all right. I pull him close and carry on holding him. If I don't let go of him he will get better.

'Did they arrest Gramps as well as you?' he asks.

'No,' I whisper.

'Why just you?'

'I came by myself to take you home.'

'You came here – what – through the tunnel?'

'Yes,' I say.

'Are you bonkers?'

'Maybe.'

He laughs. A wheezy laugh. At least I made him see the funny side.

'Standish, what crazy, brave idea were you thinking of?'

'A good one,' I said.

Though I have to admit the guard was right when he said I was lucky. Finding Hector was the best bit of luck so far. Maybe it's a sign that this might all work out. All I need is the belief it can.

Hector says softly, 'I've thought a lot about you.'

'I'm taking you to the land of Croca-Colas,' I say. 'Remember? We are going to drive one of those big Cadillacs.'

'What colour is it?' he asks, and this worries me. Hector should remember. We talked about it often enough.

'Sky blue,' I say.

He coughs. Not a good sound. Too deep, too full of coffins.

Why is mankind so fucking cruel?

Why?

Eighty-Eight

The lights go off.

'They do this all the time – on, off, on, off. It's supposed to drive you mad. I feel it might be working,' says Hector.

I don't want him thinking gloomy thoughts. But nothing sounds that cheerful in the dark of this tin can.

'Does it hurt?' I ask. 'Your hand?'

'Yes. No,' he says.

He rests his head against me. He is burning up. I was going to tell him about my stone but now all I can think of is us escaping from here. We need to find Mr Lush. Hector needs medicine.

I wish I could see his face. All I can hear is that snake rattle in his chest.

Words mask the noise.

I say, 'When you left, there was this huge hole. I couldn't walk around with a hole that size in the heart of me.'

He says nothing but I know he is listening. Words are the only medicine I have.

'You make sense of a world that is senseless. You gave me space boots so that I could walk on other planets. Without you, I'm lost. There's no left, no right. No tomorrow, only miles of yesterdays. It doesn't matter what happens now because I've found you. That's why I'm here. Because of you. You who I love. My best friend. My brother.'

Hector says, sleepily, 'I should never have gone searching for the football.'

There is nothing I can say to that. All I can see is the emptiness between his words.

His voice trails off. He is asleep. The only sound is the sand grater of his rasping breath.

Eighty-Nine

I wake with a start. For a moment I have no idea where I am. The lights are on again. The door is thrown open and the guard who looks like Mr Gunnell enters with a tray of food. He puts it down before me. This is real food – the smell is mouth-watering.

'Eat!'

I take the tray over to Hector.

'No. Just you.'

'I won't,' I say. 'Not unless he can eat as well.'

The guard slaps me round the head.

'I order you to eat.'

I think I am in for one mighty beating. Hector moves deeper into the corner, imprinting himself on the wall. I can tell that the guard is itching to break my head. I can see his thoughts running round his flabby brain. But I'm gambling that he hasn't been given those instructions yet. That will come after the astronaut has landed on the moon and the world has eaten the tea tray. My heart only starts to beat again when the guard leaves, taking the tray of food with him. I seem to be right about the beating. The door slams shut behind him. The enticing smell of food lingers.

'What the fricking hell are you doing?' asks Hector.

'We both eat or we both don't.'

'Standish, no one in here gets food. This is no frick-fracking holiday camp.'

'I think I might have some power.'

'Oh, Standish, what is going on in that daydreaming head of yours?'

So I tell Hector about the rope and how I make the astronaut look as if he is walking without gravity. And I tell him about the giant and the stone.

Hector stares at me.

'We made a space rocket, remember?' I say. 'We were going to Planet Juniper. We nearly did. If they hadn't taken you we would be there now.'

Hector looks as if he is about to say you're crazy, but

doesn't. He tilts his head back against the wall. I see there are tears running down his face.

'You are right,' he says. 'We could have escaped in that rocket. It was my fault we didn't. I couldn't believe like you. I couldn't see beyond the cardboard. This time,' Hector says, 'this time, Standish, I believe you. All of me believes you. If anyone can throw the stone, you will. If anyone can free me from this hellhole you can.'

Ninety

We hear footsteps. The key turns in the lock. What the fuck's going to happen now? Perhaps they gave the guard permission to beat my brains in after all.

Guard One has another guard with him and behind them both is a man with a small body and a head that appears to be stuck on a pole. This man is wearing a white coat. They make Hector stand. His legs fold under him. He is thrown over the shoulder of the guard who wants to break all my bones.

'Where are you taking him?' I shout. 'Leave him alone, don't touch him.'

The man in the white coat just raises his hand.

'Put him down,' I yell. 'Leave him be, just fucking well leave him be. If you hurt him I won't do anything for you.'

I am just an insect. The second guard brushes me away so hard I land in a heap where Hector has been. The floor is wet. He's pissed himself. They all leave, slamming the door shut. I get up, throw myself at it again and again. The lights go out.

Ninety-One

I'm in the dark. Time has forgotten me. I've no idea how long I've been sitting here, me and my musical pit of an empty stomach. I think about Gramps, Miss Phillips and the moon man. I wonder if they made it out. I think about Hector and stop worrying about the tears. It's dark, who can see them anyway? My head spins with all the many possibilities of the What If game. I'm trying not to cry. I'm really trying. I have this lump in my throat, this fury choking me.

I must calm down. I must not go over the moon, not yet. Stay calm. Don't go getting moon mad. Moon sad.

Moon morons.

Who do I want to be right now, right this moment? I want to be a Juniparian. I would then with my radiant vision save Hector and all the thousands of people in here. The trouble is I have a feeling that this might be a bit too much even for Juniparians. It might be too much for me. No, I can't think like that.

But what if I have it all wrong and I don't have the power to throw my stone? It wouldn't be the first time I've got things backwards. Tomorrow they'll just find a more cooperative, terrified little squirt to hang in the harness.

I am not worried about that, not much. What worries me sick is the thought of Hector having another finger chopped off.

Ninety-Two

I nearly jump out of my shoes. The light is turned on and Guard One comes in. I'm close to insanely blurting out why I'm here. It's terror that's making me long to do it. The words are rising, a fart in my throat. I close my eyes. If he is going to kill me, best not to watch.

There is the sound of something being dragged into the cell. It makes me look. The guards are putting down two thin mattresses. Then they bring Hector back. His hand is newly bandaged, he's had a change of clothes.

He lies on the mattress, shivering.

The guard brings in two trays of food as well as a blanket. I put the blanket over Hector. He says he's freezing. But I feel his skin. He is a frying pan.

'Eat,' the guard commands.

It's fish and chips. Fish and chips with a huge wedge of lemon. This is a Zone One meal. I've never in my life seen a real lemon. I sniff the lemon. It smells of sunlight. It is the only colour in this grey cell. I eat and lick my plate. Hector hasn't touched his food.

'You've got to have something,' I say. 'It will make you better.'

I cut up his food and he takes the smallest of bits.

'You eat it for me, Standish,' he says.

I am so hungry that I do. I don't want to think about Hector being this ill. I just can't think about it, that's all. He turns his head away and closes his eyes. I eat it. I could've eaten the plate.

The guard takes away the trays. The door is locked, the light turned off.

Only the moon shines in.

'I am very cold,' says Hector. I put my arms round him, hoping he will stop shivering, hoping he will stop burning up.

'I saw my father,' Hector whispers into my ear.

'Good.'

'He knew you were here. He asked if the moon man had reached you.'

'No,' I say.

The old Hector would never have let me get away with that. I have never kept anything from Hector before, only this, and I feel ashamed. But what if he knew, and they were going to chop off another finger? I know what I would do. I would spew it all out. Best to keep it to myself.

I think Hector is asleep when he says, 'I don't believe you.'

Ninety-Three

Nothing matters except Hector. He is the moment, this moment. He is the only moment.

'Kiss me,' he says softly.

I always imagined that the first person I would kiss would be a girl. Now it doesn't matter. I kiss him. The kiss is returned with longing. A longing for a life we will never have.

'I love you,' he whispers. 'The crazy, brave muddle that is you.'

I say, 'Hector, just stay with me. I can't do this without you.'

'I will be with you,' he says. 'I won't leave you. I promise. I never break a promise.'

We fall asleep, wrapped up in each other.

I wake up, terrified. Someone is untangling us. Two men in white coats. They pull me up off the mattress. I stand back, dazed. They are bending over Hector, listening to his chest.

'What's wrong?'

'Move away,' says a white-coated man.

I take no notice. One of the men is speaking in the Mother Tongue to his colleague. I don't want to hear what they are saying. I know it isn't good. I can see it isn't good. Just one look at Hector tells me that. His face is grey.

'Hector . . .' I say.

'Standish . . .'

His breathing is all wrong.

A guard comes to take me out. A white coat stops him. I kneel down beside Hector. He whispers in my ear.

'I am going to find that ice-cream-coloured Cadillac.'

I don't get time to reply. The guards have the patience of a gnat. I'm pulled to my feet, I'm fighting them, I don't fricking care what they do to me.

'Hector,' I shout. 'Wait – don't go without me . . .'

Mr Lush is running down the corridor. I don't think he sees me. He has aged about a hundred years. His hair has gone from grey to white. He is with Hector even before he arrives in the cell.

I know what Hector is doing. He's escaping from here as fast as he can. If I'm honest with myself, I've known it all along. I don't blame him, I just wish he had waited for me. If this is the way the world spins I don't want to stay either.

Ninety-Four

All our lives have one day circled when we will be rubbed out. It's a good thing not to know the date. But probably no one would think it would happen like this.

Above me hangs a large red and silver flying saucer. I know what it is. You would have to be blind, deaf and daft not to know. It has been featured in every paper in the world. It's the landing craft. It will break away from the orbiting rocket and land on the lunar surface of Zone Seven.

It looks impressively useless.

I'm taken to the same trench as yesterday, in the same crease in the moon's surface. The cameras are in place – big, clumsy-looking things.

I'm clipped into the harness by the man from yesterday,

the one in the brown overalls, while sandbags are attached to me to make me the right weight. I just hope I am strong enough to unclip myself when the time comes. I can feel the belt snuggled round my waist, waiting. I haven't worked out how I'm going to take it out. That, at the moment, is my biggest problem.

From the arm of a crane floating above us the director barks out his orders. In less than an hour, maybe sooner, these pictures will be beamed to the world. Today, unlike yesterday, there are small televisions in the trench for brown overalls to see what is happening. That's a relief.

The red flying saucer whirls down to the earth-bound moon, jets of air dispersing the sand as it makes a flawless landing. If this was really happening the astronaut inside would be fried. You might hope the free world would have worked that out for itself but I think it prefers the spine-chiller theory that all is within man's grasp.

Ninety-Five

With a jerk I feel the weight at the other end of the wire and my feet leave the ground as the astronaut takes a small jump on to the moon surface.

'Cut,' shouts the man in the crane. 'Where is the footprint?

A panic-stricken man brings the cast of a boot. It's quite a rigor mortis to place it exactly at the right spot. People with cloths covering their shoes take careful measurements then lay the footprint just where the astronaut should first place his space boot. Brown overalls tells me exactly where I need to be in the trench when the astronaut comes out of the landing craft. We practise this again and again. Then there is more fuss about the right place to put the flag. That flag is the sticking point, I can tell you.

As a warm-up I am pulled up and down by the man in the overalls until I get the hang of it. All the markers are in to tell me where to land and when to jump. The astronaut in his huge helmet still can't see the hole that's been specially made for the flag. They use a rock to mark where Y meets X. The flag flops. I mean, it could be any old red and black flag.

'Cut,' says the director.

Ninety-Six

Finally, it is time. I'm more nervous than I have ever been. If I blow this then everything will have been for naught. The astronaut is helped back into the landing craft and the whole thing is hoisted up again into the blacked-out roof. Better, I think, that the real moon doesn't see this – it might fall out the sky with laughter. Only it isn't funny. And I am still worrying how I'm going to get my belt off from under my clothes. Still haven't thought what I will do after I have shown the world my sign.

My heart sinks to the hole in the sole of my shoe. In a glass-panelled observation room I see a figure that I recognise and it is the leather-coat man. I know he is looking for me. This could mean one of two things:

either Gramps, Miss Phillips and the moon man didn't escape, or they did escape and the leather-coat man has found the tunnel.

I keep low in my trench. The man in the brown overalls who has been with me all the time climbs out. I see it doesn't take him long to scramble over the top. He starts arguing about the use of a wind machine as there is no atmosphere on the moon and the flag wouldn't blow about. Desperately, I scrabble to release Gramps' belt, to find the ribbon so that I can just whisk it out when the time comes. I breathe again when the knot comes loose. He has designed it well. The ribbon is within my grasp. I can see the feet of a guard. He isn't concentrating on me, though I am sure that's what he is supposed to be doing. No, too interested in watching the landing craft being winched into place. The guard's feet are joined by a pair of well-polished boots. I look up again at the observation room but the leather-coat man isn't there. He is standing right here with his back to me. He is asking the guard if he has seen a young boy, about fifteen, with different-coloured eyes.

Frick-fracking hell. I'm so close and now I'm going to be caught.

'What are you doing?' shouts the man in the brown overalls at the leather-coat man. 'Get off the surface of the moon.'

'It is possible that a boy called Standish Treadwell is hiding in here? We found the remains of a tunnel.'

One of the pig-wigs in charge has come over.

'Leave,' he says. 'Now.'

'Two suspects are missing and we believe . . .' carries on the leather-coat man, 'we believe they have the missing astronaut with them.'

The pig-wig says, 'Then what are you doing here?'

My heart soars. They got away.

'Ten minutes to countdown,' booms the director from the crane.

'I suggest you go and find him,' says the pig-wig.

I think he must have clicked his fingers. Whatever he has done, the leather boots that belong to the leather-coat man have vanished.

Still, I don't trust that he has gone altogether. I am as jumpy as a bed bug.

Ninety-Seven

'The President, sir,' says a Greenfly, who has come over to where the pig-wig stands. He hands him the telephone on a long wire.

The pig-wig takes the phone, stands to attention and gives the salute of the Motherland. He doesn't say a word. Just the salute and then he hands the phone back to the guard.

'It's an order from the President,' he announces. 'The flag must wave in the breeze.'

The wind machine is pulled into position, everyone is on stand-by. The countdown begins.

For the first time I am aware Hector is near me.

'Don't worry, Standish,' he says, softly. 'We will do this together like we always did.'

'But what if they catch you here?' I say.

He smiles. 'They won't.'

I know that.

Ninety-Eight

How the fricking hell am I going to unclip the invisible wire while the guard and the man in the brown overalls have their beady eyes on me?

'Stand by,' shouts the director from his position on the crane.

The eyes of the world are tuned in to us. On a TV set a very crackly picture of the surface of the moon comes into view.

The landing craft makes a perfect touchdown, scattering the silver sand. The puffs of air are more powerful than before, strong enough to make a miniature sand storm. The man in brown overalls is riveted by the sight.

The landing craft doors slide open and there is the astronaut. He floats down the steps. The only mistake is that he lands a centimetre off the footprint, but not enough for anyone to notice.

When both feet are on the ground he says, 'This is to prove to the enemies of the Motherland that we will rule for all eternity.'

Now begins the much-practised moon walk. I can do this, I know I can. I have been thinking of nothing else since . . . since Hector's ghost came to stand beside me.

The astronaut is half jumping, half walking. I am bobbing up-down, up-down, landing on each of my markers.

Maybe it is this that makes both the Greenfly and the man in brown overalls take their eyes off me. They are glued to the TV.

The astronaut is unfolding the flag. One more leap, then he is in the right position.

Hector says, 'Now, Standish, now.'

That's when I unclip the wire. That's when I make my move.

Ninety-Nine

The astronaut who has been enjoying the false sense of weightlessness tumbles, stumbles, falls, drops the flag. I reckon I have than less than thirty seconds before I am caught. I scramble up the steps, out of the trench. I have the belt in my hand.

Hector is with me. I stand in front of the camera and stretch the belt out so that Gramps' words can be seen. Maybe even he can see them. I hope so.

It starts with one weak voice.

And did those feet in ancient time . . .

Then other voices join in. The voices of all the workers fill this slaughterhouse.

Walk upon England's mountains green . . .

One Hundred

For a moment the Greenflies, the leather-coat man and the pig-wigs stand speechless. This is my moment. Not even one minute, just a moment. But maybe all it needs is a moment to change the course of history. I am on the moon. I am the stone. The plug is pulled on the maggot moon.

The machine guns begin to fire, the shells rain around me like shooting stars. I just hope the world saw me. I just hope I've thrown myself hard enough into the nightmare that is the Motherland. People are running in every direction inside that atrocity of a building. Hector is waving to me – I know he has found the way out. Mr Lush is coming towards me.

'Can you see him?' I ask. 'He's over there.'

'Who?' he says.

'Hector.'

We weave in and out of the panicking crowd, until Hector shows me the door. I push the bar down and we are out into the dawn of a new day. Before us Zone Seven is rising from the mist.

Mr Lush has hold of me, unsure what to do.

'Follow Hector,' I say and point down the hill. We run away, roll away, throw ourselves on to the grass. Only now do I see the blood. It is coming from me.

'I did it, I fricking did it, didn't I?'

'You did, Standish, you did it,' says Mr Lush. 'Just hold on.'

I know I'm in trouble. And I think I have held on long enough.

'Stay with me, Standish, you will be all right.'

Mr Lush's voice seems to be from a distant planet.

It is Hector who pulls me to my feet. He has found a car, a huge, ice-cream-coloured Cadillac. I can smell the leather. Bright blue, sky blue, leather seats blue. Hector sits in the back. Me with my arm resting on the chrome of the wound-down window, my hand on the wheel. I am driving us home to Mrs Lush in her shiny kitchen with a checked tablecloth in a house where the grass looks as if it's been Hoovered.

You see, only in the land of Croca-Colas does the sun shine in Technicolor. Life lived at the end of the rainbow.